Y0-DKL-852

Ocean of Mercy

Atoma Živ

Oxygentribe Press

© Atoma Živ 1999

l

All rights reserved.
No portion of this book may be reproduced or utilized in
any form or by any means, electronic or mechanical,
without prior permission in writing from the publisher.

Published by
Oxygentribe Press
P.O. Box 460387
San Francisco, CA 94146-0387

Printed in the United States of America

artwork and design by Atoma Živ

Library of Congress Card Number: 99-067732

ISBN 0967476526

"Mercy and truth are met together; righteousness and peace have kissed each other." (Psalm 85:10)

Venus in Scorpio:
I have been anointed.
Open the floodgates
of my womb,
touch with your hands
my Sacred Heart,
for I am
the Mystery,
the Resurrection,
and the Love.

1. Immersion
2. Confession
3. Renunciation
4. Imagination
5. Evolution
6. Initiation (inhalation)
7. Purification (exhalation)
8. Celebration
9. Crucifixion
10. Transmutation
11. Resurrection
12. Destination

Renunciation

Purification

Transmutation

Resurrection

1. Immersion

pure   2. Free from adulterants or impurities; full strength. 3. Free from dirt, defilement or pollution; clean. 5. Containing nothing inappropriate or extraneous. 6. Complete; thorough; utter. 7. Without faults; perfect; sinless.

shadow   7. A mirrored image or reflection. 10. A faint indication; premonition. 11. A vestige; remnant. 13.Shelter; protection. -tr. v. 3. To represent vaguely, mysteriously, or prophetically.

I was born during the war, born into a world of blood and brightness, born of a frightened woman into the hands of frightened men, people at war. While in my mother's womb, her blood brought me messages from the secret places in her heart and whispered to me of her fear and of the world I would be joining.

There was no sentimentality over a birth. My mother and I could no longer inhabit the same body and had to be separated. It was time. She needed help and it was done. The floor was full of her blood, but she survived and so did I.

In the beginning, with no differentiation between myself and others, grief ran through me like light, air, and mother's milk, the pain of the "holy war." Unable as yet to choose, only to feel, what touched me was the strong, dark, screaming presence of war.

Living and breathing in a continual state of terror, I was surrounded by burning and rotting flesh, bathed in streams of blood gone lifeless, immersed in agony that would not cease. Funereal wailing woke me from every nap and each day showed me living flesh torn and crumpled as casually as paper, continuously and relentlessly.

I really don't know how I survived initially. It mystified me, this deep, tenacious desire to live no matter what. I could not fathom why I wanted to remain in this nightmare but I did.

My parents fussed quite a bit over what they considered to be my tardy development. Apparently they didn't realize I was in a state of shock for the first years of my life. Though somewhere close to the age of three I did begin to speak a little, I remained a fairly quiet child.

I took my cue from my parents, who never acknowledged the war. They seemed uncomfortable with my tentative attempts at questioning, and from this I inferred that it was a subject not to be spoken about. I found most of what they did speak of nonsensical, and began to suspect that there must be some kind of code that I needed to interpret.

Language was not so simple, after all. Their background emotions made sense: anxiety, fear, hostility, rage, grief; but the inane conversations of trivia and gossip while next to us a whole family was blasted to nothing? It was a relief to grasp the concept of code but it didn't help me much, just gave me a direction in which to struggle.

Carnage raged around us and yet we sat at dinner in relative calm. What protected us? Who was saving us? What made us different from the others, the victims? I cursed my inability to comprehend, to solve the mystery and answer my questions.

One morning when I was about five years old, I awoke to the sound of birdsong outside my window. The morning was different because of what was absent: missiles, bullets, wailing, dying. The playful spirit that had trembled inside me for five long years leapt up in joy. The war was over!

Weeping in gratitude, my senses reached out in delirious happiness to seize it all: the sunlight filling my room with warmth and light, the laughter of birdsong, the soft comfort of my childhood bed, the quiet beating of my heart. I stayed in my room alone for a long time, breathing deeply and fully for the first time in my life, savoring the clean taste of air unpolluted by poison gas. Five years I had waited to fill my lungs completely, five long years of yearning and hunger. My limbs stretched out and relaxed. My flesh no longer flinched in empathetic pain with flesh melted by chemical torture. To rest and breathe that morning was the most precious and nourishing event of my childhood.

When I emerged to greet my parents, they baffled me with their lack of celebration. Since the war was a subject we never discussed, I waited throughout the day, alert and watchful for some change in them. At last, confused and frustrated, I decided to be direct and went to my father as he took his after dinner cigarette in his big armchair.

I told him I knew the war was over and endured the condescending way he mussed my hair and patted my cheek. Then, sighing, he took me onto his lap and wrapped his big arms around me. We sat in silence for a few moments, then he told me that the war was far from over, but that was not for me to think about at my age.

I panicked. Was I losing my senses? Could this be the beginning of paralysis, mental illness, or even death? My father spoke to me with the soothing tones a parent uses when a child has had a bad dream. He explained that the war was far, far away and that I could never have heard, seen or felt it. My mother, watching me, nodded her agreement with what my father was saying, a bemused look in her eyes.

The war was not over. It was in another part of the world. It was expected that no one feel it. Somehow distance was supposed to obliterate it, to smother its noxious presence like a blanket smothering fire. I knew in my heart that this could not be, that the raw-nerve cruelty of the mass death was strong enough to seize every living being and choke them with the sights and the sounds and the pain.

Unless...

Unless there was something wrong with the senses. Unless there was something wrong with the brain. Unless there was something wrong and sick and putrid in the heart. My guts turned over and I understood. Such a person was my father. Such a person was my mother. And now, such a person was I.

It didn't take long for me to review my harsh assessment of my situation. This state of psychic slumber was pleasant; from this perspective, life had many fine things to offer.

My best friend was the sky, vast and blue, a unique entity whose every thought was a cloud. If this being could embrace the world and contemplate us with such serenity perhaps I could learn from it. Hours would pass while I lay on my back watching the clouds promenade through the sky, changing from dancers to castles to mountains to mermaids to dragons to angels. I could remain mesmerized by the magical parade of the heavens without any disturbance except my mother calling me to dinner.

My parents' conversations could be taken at face value and participated in without searching for hidden meanings. Sometimes I wondered what it meant to be separated from other people in this way, to be deaf and blind to both the suffering and the presence of others, but it was such an easy way to live that I rapidly grew accustomed to it.

The gates were not completely shut, however, and from time to time my senses opened a bit to bring me vivid dreams and episodes of what they called sleepwalking. I would walk into my parents' bedroom and see my mother wrestling with phantoms, her belly a bubbling, burning cauldron.

My parents were at war with each other. Was it the strong presence of the war running through them, were they trapped together in their own private war, or was it even possible to differentiate between the

15

two?

Perhaps everyone was emotionally contaminated by the war, no matter how much we closed our senses to it. Perhaps everyone ate and drank the pain of the war every day, and all we did in our relationships was vomit. As the presence of the war receded further into memory, such thoughts became increasingly philosophical exercises, devoid of emotion.

My father was filled with sadness from all he had lost to the plague, while my mother was enraged for reasons she never revealed to me. Her anger was the wild horse that could not stop running and his sadness was the ground she trampled. In this sense, they were a match for each other. My mother spit on my father and fed his sadness; he provided her with a target. They both grew more bitter with each passing year but, like addicts, they were unable to stay apart for very long.

As I grew, slumber became both more consistent and desirable. It seemed wise to trade awareness for the protection of the blindfold. Sometimes, when the feelings were raw and emanating strongly enough to fill the house with tension, I went for walks around the neighborhood and thought about other things, like why sidewalks were made of squares.

I had little interest in participating in the feelings of others. I understood it was not done; I understood life was easier that way. It occurred to me that I had lost something, but I had also gained something. I enjoyed the privacy of my own mind.

2. Confession

fascinate   1. To be an object of intense interest to; attract irresistibly. 2. To hold motionless; to spellbind or mesmerize. [Latin fascinare, to enchant, bewitch, from fascinus, a bewitching, amulet in the shape of a phallus.]

According to the religion I was raised with, I was born with sin on my soul. This means I was born unworthy, at fault, estranged from my Creator, in trouble, in debt with my very first breath. A specially trained man could, and did, pour water and words over me and I was made clean, ready to begin a life during which this cleansing of my soul would continue on a regular basis, like doing laundry, in hopes of having a clean soul at the moment of my death. If I were successful, an eternity of bliss with my Creator would be my reward .

The first humans, Adam and Eve, were supposedly responsible for this Original Sin, as it was called. They disobeyed their Creator, their loving and merciful Father God who could forgive all things except for the violation of one rule: not to eat the fruit of the tree that was placed temptingly within their sight. As a result of this inexcusable blunder we are now all born in sin, a potent blend of shame, guilt, and pathetic unworthiness that renders people unable to feel truth with their own hearts.

For Friday dinner my mother often prepared fillet of sole, a rather delicate, bland white fish. Due to the same-sounding names, I imagined my immortal soul to resemble this fish fillet, a bland, flat, white internal organ suspended somewhere between my heart and my stomach.

I imagined that when I committed a venial (little) sin, like lying or thinking bad thoughts about my parents, these sins were registered on my soul as grey and brown marks, leaving my soul looking in color like a pair of white sneakers after their first day out. Confession washed off these marks and prepared me for Holy Communion.

In this state, if death came, my soul would fly out of my body and join God in heaven, where I would discover just how wonderful He was and spend an eternity of bliss with Him. It was impossible to figure out if my soul would continue to look like a fish fillet or if it would change and look like me.

I couldn't imagine what a mortal sin would look like. A mortal sin, like murder, suicide, or adultery, would send a person's soul to hell to burn in fire for all eternity. Not only would a person suffer unbearable torment forever, but none of the happy souls in heaven would even care, even if they had loved you here on earth. Though God loves us all, He wouldn't care either. You have your chance. If you end up in hell, eternal punishment is obviously entirely in order, because God is just.

Then, of course, there were the unfortunates who bumbled along, doing their best, committing occasional venial sins. What if they died without getting their souls washed and it wasn't even their fault?

They went to purgatory, which was a kind of grey zone for grey souls. They eventually went to heaven and people here could pray for them to help them along. It didn't sound like too pleasant of a place, and though there were no time estimates given for stays there, it always sounded like the soul-cleansing went on in slow motion.

More nebulous than purgatory was limbo, which means "region on the border of hell." This is where people went who weren't baptized. My understanding of it was that people didn't suffer there like in hell, but they couldn't go to heaven either. To me it sounded like an eternity of boredom, which seemed hellish enough. I guess that's why it's on hell's border.

That's the geography of the afterlife. It made sense to try to get to heaven. What I was taught about accomplishing that was the strangest thing of all.

I was taught there were two ways to get to heaven: one was to love God, in which case you were happily subservient to His will and after death your affinity and love carried you to Heaven. If you found yourself unable to love God for whatever reason, (in my case, because this maze we were to run seemed nonsensical and mean-spirited; therefore, I was suspicious of its source), there was another option: to live a good life because you were afraid of God and His punishments. Either way would work! Love or fear, take your pick; both lead to the same reward!

Later in life I experimented with this love/fear concept, falling in love with tortured, sensitive souls (men) who needed the love of a good woman (me) to heal their psychic wounds and melt away their pain. Inevitably the violence of their pain frightened me deeply, the love of a (trying-to-be-) good woman failed and the situation degenerated into one of brutality. Love and fear never lead to the same place. I have researched this thoroughly and am sure this is true.

The hero of our religion was Jesus Christ, who died for our sins. He was the only son of God, who healed the sick, raised the dead, showed the way to the Kingdom of Heaven (Within us! Not just after we die!) forgave the frightened people who murdered him, spent three days bringing light to the dead in hell and finally resurrecting himself in glory before ascending to Heaven.

Someone who did all that had to be a spectacular guy, but our church didn't talk about that much. The central focus was his suffering and death, keeping alive our collective guilt at needing the son of God to suffer unimaginable pain to save us from our spiritual ineptitude. We were surrounded by pictures and statues of Jesus on the cross, of Jesus wearing a crown of thorns and sweating blood, of Jesus falling beneath the burden of his cross, also known as our sins. Had it worked, his great sacrifice? Were we any closer to finding the Kingdom of Heaven he talked about? It sure didn't seem like it. We always had to bow our heads when we said the name of Jesus.

Jesus Christ was different because his mother was a virgin so he was born without sin. I inferred from this that sin could be transmitted like a venereal disease. Sometimes it seemed like God had made a few mistakes, sex being one of them, people another. Jesus was supposedly different from all of us, but he said "Greater things than I have done, you shall do, because I go to the Father" (John 14:12). Why weren't we doing them?

He said, "Peace I leave with you, my peace I give unto you. Let not your heart be troubled, neither let it be afraid" (John 14:27). Why were we sniveling and unworthy? Why were the majority of our thoughts and words nothing more than rabid fear foaming from our mouths? Why were we bound for hell unless someone saved us? I pondered these matters deeply, because they perplexed me. I never doubted the truth of immortality, the soul, the afterlife, God, or Jesus Christ. I knew for certain that all this existed, I just wasn't sure if it existed in quite the way it was taught to me.

However, I was small and the Church was big, so I couldn't just dismiss what they told me, especially since eternity was at stake. I no more wanted to suffer forever than the next person, so I didn't want to make any rash decisions. I needed to investigate and contemplate what I learned there.

The summer of my eighth birthday we visited my aunt in the north. I learned of the strength of nature's emotions and fell in love with thunderstorms that year. Before a storm hit, the air would fill with a palpable stillness. The tiger lilies in the neighbor's garden would quiver in their communion with that magnetism and power, and I, fascinated, would watch them closely, savoring the charged air.

Once, just before a storm, I caught a butterfly because that's what children my age did and it was important to be like my peers. I put it in a glass jar with holes punched in the top and put some grass in with it to give the jar a semblance of home. That night I went to bed but was unable to fall asleep. I listened to the rain outside, steadily drumming on the window, the gentle aftermath of lightning and thunder.

There was a weight on my chest; I could not get comfortable. My thoughts were chaotic and restless; I tossed and turned and finally located the source of my discomfort. I got up, flung open the window and released the butterfly from its jar prison. I apologized to it and went back to my bed, feeling untroubled and ready to sleep. I felt good about this experience. It meant my conscience was in good working order.

I did not want this to change. I decided I did not want to go to heaven, oblivious to the suffering of all those condemned to hell. I did not want to go to hell either, or anyplace in between. I decided I would go somewhere else. I didn't know where else there was in the afterlife, but I knew there must be a place for people who didn't want anyone to suffer. Maybe there was a different God there.

In our religion, we got in touch with God's grace through the sacraments. Some of the sacraments were usually performed only once in a lifetime: Baptism, Confirmation, Matrimony or Holy Orders (becoming a priest or nun) and Extreme Unction (the last cleansing before you die).

Confession and Holy Communion, however, were available on a regular basis: Confession to cleanse your soul and prepare you for Communion, and Communion to receive the body of Jesus Christ in the form of a little wafer called the Host. It was a sin to go to Communion without first going to Confession or to eat before Communion. We usually received Communion in the morning and sometimes I felt faint without breakfast.

It was against the rules to chew the Host. I suppose that would have been a sign of disrespect. Somehow it didn't seem all that respectful to have Jesus' body slowly melting in my mouth either. I never had any special feelings after taking the Host. I wanted to. I enjoyed the rituals, the incense, the candles and the form of the Mass, so I wanted the heart of the Mass to have meaning for me. Usually it was just an embarrassment to kneel before the priests and altar boys, many of whom were my classmates, with my mouth open and my tongue hanging out. It disappointed me that girls could not participate in the Mass the way the priests and altar boys did.

I remember Confession and the tightness in my chest when I entered the dark box, feeling claustrophobia and fear, reciting meaningless things I had been told to say, such as "I disobeyed my mother three times." There could be no virtue in these parrotlike litanies. One day I resolved to really talk about something and explore myself inside the dark box of the confessional despite my nervousness.

"Bless me Father, for I have sinned. It has been two weeks since my last Confession."

My heart was slamming against my skin so hard I thought the sound must surely be audible to the priest on the other side of the partition. I opened my mouth to say "I disobeyed my parents three times" and forget my plan, but somehow I found myself saying, "Father, I don't know if what I have done is a sin or not. I had a boyfriend, Glen Kibsey. We used to go to the lake after school and walk around, sometimes kiss. Last month was especially nice because the lilacs were out. I love the smell of lilacs more than anything else in the world. We would lay down under them and kiss. It was wonderful except for one thing.

"He had a friend, Robert, who would come with us and follow us around. He would sit down a ways away from us, but I couldn't always forget about him and it was kind of weird, like he was watching us. I asked Glen if we could just go by ourselves but he said Robert was his friend and he didn't want him to feel bad.

"I didn't care. I didn't like him very much. He never said anything, just followed us around. I think boyfriends and girlfriends should be alone together sometimes. Anyway, Glen wouldn't get rid of him, so I just tried to ignore him.

"Last week Glen asked me to come to his house on Saturday morning. I went over there and he was in the back waiting for me. Robert was there, too. Glen asked me to swear not to tell anyone what we were going to do, not even my mother. I didn't want to swear that, because I like to tell my mother things, but he said we wouldn't do it unless I swore and I was really curious, so I swore.

"We went inside the shed, all three of us. It was small and dark in there, kind of like in here, in the confessional. Glen pulled down his pants and asked me to pull mine down too, so I did. Then he kissed me and put his thing between my legs. Robert said we had to stay like that for two minutes. That didn't seem very long to me. I liked kissing Glen and he felt warm and nice between my legs. Robert had a watch with him and he watched the time. I figured they just did that to make up a job for him.

"After two minutes Robert told us to stop. Glen pulled his pants up. I was thinking maybe Robert could leave now and we could do it some more without timing it. Then they told me they wanted me to do it with Robert! I said, "No! Never!" I wouldn't. They both ran out of the shed and locked me in. They told me they wouldn't let me out until I did it with Robert so I said, "okay," and they opened the door.

"I went and put my arms around Robert's neck. He's taller than me. I went to kiss him and bit him as hard as I could on his bottom lip. I was happy when I stepped back and saw all the blood on his lip and the surprised look on his face. I told Glen I never wanted to see him again and ran home. The next day Glen came over but I meant what I said. I told him to get lost. I think he was a real creep.

"What do you think, Father? Did I sin? I know we're not supposed to hurt anybody but I really felt good biting Robert's lip. Was it wrong to pull down my pants for Glen? I thought I loved him, but I don't, at least not anymore. Was it wrong for me to swear not to tell anyone and then come in here and tell you?"

I sat back, waiting to hear Father Jacobson's response. I felt a surge of power at my boldness in talking about my boyfriend in Confession.

"I want you to go into our Lady's chapel. Say the rosary, not as a penance but as a prayer for understanding. Pray to know what is right for you."

This was new! I was excited by the thought of praying to know what was right for me, not just swallowing dogma. I smiled in the darkness.

"Thank you, Father."

26

His hand made the sign of the cross.

"Peace be with you," he said and closed the partition.

Our Lady's chapel was small and off to the side of the church, near the area of the confessionals. Inside was a statue of Mary looking young and holy in her blue gown. There was hardly ever anyone there, but I had always liked it.

Kneeling down in front of the statue, I took out my rosary beads, which were a present from my godfather, made of wood from the Holy Land. I liked the feel of them better than plastic rosary beads. The wood was smooth and warmed quickly from my touch. When I heard someone enter the chapel, I wanted to look but also wanted to appear as if I were truly praying and not easily distracted, so I managed not to turn my head. Then I heard the door close and lock.

"It's me," Father Jacobson said. "I've come to pray with you. You don't need to turn around."

Something in his voice excited me. I heard a sound for the first time, a sound that I came to expect and enjoy, the sound of his robe swishing as he moved it aside while he knelt down behind me, raised the back of my skirt and put his stiff willie between my thighs. What a difference between his and Glen's! His was a man's, not a boy's, penis. It was strong and firm, quivering and jumping between my legs with a personality of its own. I liked it very much.

Father Jacobson and I prayed the entire rosary this way, praying out loud with his voice deep and close to my ear, swaying together as we knelt there. It was thrilling. He was initiating me into God's love.

We prayed the rosary together after almost every Confession. I would come to church during the quiet time, late Thursday afternoon, and would always try to be last, but sometimes someone would go in after me. I would go to the chapel and pray alone, waiting, alert, wondering if Father Jacobson would be able to join me and if so, when. My anticipation throbbed through my body and every sound in the quiet church stirred me, my body begging for him.

His arrival would satisfy the longing of waiting for him, but his presence and his touch aroused new sensations of even greater intensity. One day while he prayed the rosary with me, he used his hand to press his willie up against me. He rubbed it back and forth until I thought I would cry or wet my pants! It felt so good I could hardly

27

hold on to my rosary. The next time I went to Confession I asked him to always do that.

I lived for going to church at that time. Everything excited me. I relished walking by the confessionals when I came to Mass. They would be empty at that time, but they seemed to hold our secret in their silence. I wondered what other secrets were held in them, for that is the essence of Confession that I had come to adore: secrecy.

My rosary was another special friend. I would grow warm and wet between my legs whenever I knelt down with my rosary. Even the sight of someone else praying with a rosary would arouse me.

Every Sunday I received Holy Communion. I would go to the 11:00 a.m. Mass, which was said by Father Jacobson. Trembling while kneeling at the altar, opening my mouth and putting out my tongue to receive the Host, I no longer felt the embarrassment I had once known, submissive and vulnerable before the priests and the altar boys.

Father Jacobson was my bridge to God and I held nothing back in his presence, yielding completely to the feelings inside me. The Host that Father Jacobson put in my mouth reminded me of his penis that he put under my skirt, between my legs. Sometimes when I felt the Host in my mouth it was as if I were tasting his penis. Now I felt the touch of God at Holy Communion.

We talked of many things in Confession and I loved being in the confessional, but it was just a doorway into the greater Mysteries. We didn't linger there. My penance was always a rosary.

This went on for several exquisite, ecstatic months. Then, one day, I was with Father Jacobson in the chapel. He was kneeling behind me in our usual way. His penis was especially animated and his voice was hoarse.

Without warning, he opened my legs further and rammed his cock into the opening in my body that I was only dimly aware of. It hurt and I begged him to stop, but he put his hand over my mouth and thrust into me violently. I tried to move away, but his strong arms held my body tightly. "I am not ready for this," my body cried out to him as I felt his betrayal, as all the pleasure in my body turned into pain. He was done with me quickly and left without a word.

I tidied up my uniform and washed my face at the holy water font. Then, feeling angry and bold, I took off my underpants, all bloody from me and sticky from him, and used them to wash myself off. When I was done I left my underpants in the holy water font and went home.

I had not escaped the shame that I had suspected waited for me in all the dogma and sacraments of Catholicism. I felt ashamed of myself, my body, my gender, what I had done and what had been done to me. I was no initiate and this was no sacrament. I had been used, tricked. My sweet memories turned bitter. I bothered my parents incessantly until they gave me permission to attend public school. I never went to church again. I was ten years old.

3. Renunciation

"What we will be has not yet been revealed." (1 John 3:2)

In my early years, I had been keenly and painfully aware of the suffering caused by the war. That time was followed by years of slumber during which I played, dreamed, learned and grew, but my senses remained operational only within the narrow limits approved by my culture. This way of being was strengthened by my religious training and my early sex experience, which suggested that it was inappropriate, even dangerous, to explore myself or my world.

That changed when I began to menstruate. Despite the teaching that it was dirty and shameful, the feel and sight of my first blood was powerful enough to strip away any such ideas from the surface of my mind. I knew that what I was experiencing was no less than the raw creative power of the universe and once again my senses opened up, this time to the sensuality of nature.

Though at first I was touched only by fragments and shadows filtering through the shame, guilt, and fear in me, I soon became more open and receptive. Every falling leaf was a kiss, every breeze a caress. Life was courting me, wooing the power within me that could create more life.

I marvelled at the delicacy of my psyche. At that time my early memories of the war were hidden from me, but I was certain that the bitterness of my mother's womb had deeply affected me in some way, while Father Jacobson had contaminated me with his religious guilt when he penetrated me. Those two bodies who had been one with mine had taught me: more than teaching, they had tuned my awareness to specific frequencies. Now my own body was teaching and healing me.

It was difficult to be around my parents. They moved together inside a dark stormy cloud. Though I loved them both, their relationship frightened me. They looked like animals caught in a trap. Each was the trap for the other and they both bled, my mother in a panic, my father resigned. It was messy. Their fights, waking me in the middle of the night, constricted my belly in fear. I wanted to run away from the emotional violence of their relationship. Often, I found myself wishing they would separate.

For the most part I was afraid of people and did not fit in well. During the times that home was in a state of relative calm, I lived for the hours of solitude in my room, flying away with the night, clad in dreams and silk, almost angelic, so soft no one could catch me.

I developed a secret monthly ritual. At night I lay naked in my bed and painted my face and body with menstrual blood, decorating and pleasuring myself, pretending to be a tribal warrior. I didn't know much about the tribes then, other than that they were nomadic and different from us.

Fantasies about them filled my days. I imagined that I was secretly one of them and that one day, being drawn to me telepathically, they would come and take me away from the boredom of school, away to the mystery of the desert where they would teach me magical ways of living.

Time passed; summer came and I was thirteen years old. The evenings were warm and often I heard strange, compelling music coming from down the street. My heart was drawn to the music and I spent many evenings sitting on our porch, experiencing a longing I could not define. I was happy in a dreamy way. The warmth of the summer nights seemed to melt into and become a component of the music, enhancing my adolescent mood.

As sometimes happens with dreams that are cherished but not grasped, mine had come true after a fashion. Several tribal families had moved in down the street. It was their music that mesmerized me. Eventually I grew bold enough to follow my longing and go to them. They allowed me in to their back yard evenings and let me dance with them. I danced with old women, with boys younger than myself, in twos, threes, or alone, it didn't matter at all. They accepted me as I might have taken in a stray kitten. They didn't fuss over me or question me. Their attitude seemed to be that if I was there, I belonged there.

At least that's how I interpreted it. They spoke little of my language, and theirs was one I had never heard before. They let me dance, they danced with me, the musicians at times caught my eye with a twinkle and a smile, and they never sent me away. Often times I would go home and make a pretense of going to sleep, then return and dance by the fire for hours, caught up in a kind of trance.

My parents, along with all the other adults I knew, feared the tribes. They feared them for the color of their skin, they feared them for their way of being at home everywhere and nowhere, for their wandering ways. They feared them for their wild laughter and their extravagant mannerisms. They feared them for their tattooed faces and because they represented the unknown. In short, they feared them for all the reasons I loved them. I wasn't foolish. I kept my visits

36

to them a strict secret.

All too soon, in spite of my stealth, my parents followed me and found me there. They were furious and, in their rage, shut me in the closet for three days as punishment. I didn't mind all that much. Solitude never bothered me. I slowed myself down, pretending to be a stone, a piece of the earth, and allowed the stillness of the dark to enter my mind, letting time pass as it would. When I was let out, the light hurt my eyes. It reminded me of Jesus Christ and his three days in the tomb. I felt the beginning of kinship with Him.

I also felt the ending of my relationship with my family as I had known it. Though it was three years before I was ready to leave home, those years we lived in our own worlds, polite strangers but strangers nonetheless.

At that time, in the egocentric way of children who think they are no longer children, I blamed them for their lack of understanding. Now, many years later, I can feel gratitude for all their efforts on my behalf, for time has taught me a little. Whatever I may have perceived as their personal failings, they gave me life and cared for me the best they knew. It is no small gift.

In the fourteen years between the time I left home and the time I wish to speak of, I travelled a great deal in the desert, which was infinitely beautiful to me. I wanted to live the life of a free spirit, but I did not feel free. I saw the beauty of the desert, of the night time sky, of the sun and the moon, of the seasons and the waters, but the beauty of people I could not see.

I took men as lovers, approaching them in the same way as I had been taught to approach God the Father: with love and fear. The two were deeply entangled in me, and where one went the other followed.

The first man I lived with had the emotional development of a two-year-old, like many others I've met since, and when I say that I mean no disrespect. The emotions of the very young are pure and intense in their honesty and whole body expression, but often as people grow, they are taught emotional inhibition in lieu of emotional maturity, and here, I believe, lies the root of many problems.

Our life together followed a common pattern. In public he was a

gentle man whom everyone admired. In the privacy of our relationship he frequently exploded in violent tantrums. Initially we both
fought and made love with a great intensity, but the fights became
violent, our lovemaking hostile, and the relationship, exhausting.

My fear of his violence paralyzed me for some time. I lived in
isolation, knowing myself only through his eyes. When I finally fled,
he pursued me. I was lost and frightened and depended on the good
will of others, often strangers. My saviours came in many forms, in
unexpected ways. In time, I learned to recognize and avoid
venomous serpents, many of whom tried to approach me in the guise
of lovers. It took longer to purge the venom in myself, since I was
accustomed to its taste.

Slowly I learned to differentiate between self-abandon and self-
destruction, between surrender and martyrdom, between yielding
and giving up. My religious training unravelled under the pressure
of life experience and I was unsure of how to find the path to my
heart. Though both love and fear were magnetic in attracting people
and situations, it became clear that they did not both lead to the
Kingdom of Heaven.

If God was my Father, then who was my Mother? If God had
created me in His image, then why did I not like myself or anyone
else I knew? Why were people brutal with their loved ones? I had
always wanted to be a saint, but it turned out there were just too
many people I couldn't stand. I couldn't save my tortured, sensitive,
violent men with the love of a good woman, nor could I help anyone
with my fear. If I couldn't be a saviour, then how would I redeem my
immortal soul? For a while, things looked pretty bleak.

It was during this time that I met the poet, who was the one truly
harmless person I met during those years. Whether that is a reflection of my world or of my psyche is impossible to say. He was
present for some of the events I wish to recount, but he has since been
lost to me. If he should come upon this story, I want him to know that
I love him. Without him, I cannot imagine that I would have learned
to trust other people with my heart, and so the rest of this story
would never have happened.

4. Imagination

imagination   1b. A mental image or idea. 3. The ability to deal creatively with reality.

It was the poet who told me about the city in one of his occasional letters, encouraging me to move there. When I had last seen him, his talk was full of the chemicals he had discovered and so enjoyed taking. He claimed they gave him visions, but the language of his eyes was one I didn't know.

He was becoming like the wind to me, present yet invisible. Maybe it was his mind melting away; certainly his soul had taken up residence somewhere utterly foreign to me. My fear was that he would not remain long in this world, and I wanted to see him again.

He had always been a true friend, and during the time we were lovers, he had created poems for me, poems with all the delicate splendor of butterfly wings. He never wrote them down and I found them effortlessly planted in my memory. That was the kind of relationship we once had, a long time ago.

I thought that now we probably wouldn't see each other much even if we were both living in the city. Still, it was pleasant to have one friendship that had survived the years of my travels. In the end, it was a gut feeling that decided me and in the last days of autumn I followed him west.

The new city was the same as any other, but the old city immediately captivated me with its walls, gates, and serpentine paths. The gleaming minarets piercing the sky and the temples nesting on the high hills spoke of timeless mysteries, while the gargoyles cried out to each other in painfully foreign voices, forever beyond the reach of human ears. My arrival coincided with the beginning of a particularly rainy winter, which only contributed to the old city's enigmatic atmosphere.

I found work on a collective farm where my efforts would serve to feed the old city's inhabitants. The work as well as the people on the farm appealed to me, the ancient beauty of the old city enthralled me, and for the first time in my adult life I thought I would be pleased to stay awhile, so I signed a five-year collective contract.

Though I had some experience in agriculture, I learned much at the farm due to the variety of crops cultivated there: wheat, corn, cotton, potatoes, sunflowers, orchards of oranges, pecans, and carob, as well as a wide variety of greens, aromatic herbs and flowers. The housing was a large honeycomb with communal areas for food and play.

Initially, I had a small room on the ground floor, but I got lucky and soon moved into a larger room on the top floor. Windows on both the south and west sides made it sunny and airy, a spacious nest with a feeling of freedom despite its walls.

I went to the market and bought a trunk for my few possessions and a piece of amber gauze. Returning to my room, I took the door off the closet and hung the gauze over the doorway. Filling the floor of the closet with blankets that were available for residents, I made myself a cozy nest. I slept in the closet turned grotto, the rest of the room empty except for my little trunk and a tribal rug I found in the market.

The first month was taken up with settling in and getting to know the farm, the people and the schedules. After that, what free time I had was spent wandering the streets of the old city, which was a baffling and fascinating maze.

Walking for hours at a time, moving slowly through the evenings in a quiet dream state, the whispered falling of the rain filling my mind with wordless poetry, I learned the intricacies of the labyrinth, peaceful and content with little need to speak to anyone, savoring the wet weather and my solitary discoveries.

Late one night I ended up on a dead-end street and stepped into a cafe called the Gates of Hell. Inside a woman was sitting on a small stage playing a zither and singing a ballad, singing so softly it was as if she were alone The place was unnaturally still considering how packed it was.

> "When I consulted the oracle about you
> I was wandering in the Gobi with bare feet
> Drenched in thoughts that could never
> Taste like water
> Drowning in a Mongolian kind of heat."

I was able to find an unoccupied seat at a table and sat down. The people at the table hardly acknowledged me. Everyone seemed absorbed in their own reverie. I ordered tea.

> "Were my eyeballs bleeding and my
> Lips pressed to the ground?
> Kowtowing in a sunset Kalahari
> Wondering if scorpions make a sound."

She was almost invisible on the stage. The lighting was dim and she had seated herself in its shadow. It gave her song an eerie quality as it emerged from the darkness.

> "Then I consulted the oracle about you
> While riding Persian horseback through a
> Clear baptismal sky.
> Round fragrant mountains
> Made of ivory, roses, and thunder
> Past oceans that never choose to cry."

Her song meandered, her throaty voice filling the air like smoke. I closed my eyes and images passed behind them, of places and people I had known, times I had been touched by love, and other images that were strange and fantastic, all vanishing whenever I tried to grasp them, like the delightful thoughts that nestle on the edge of sleep, the kind that are impossible to track when one looks for their origin .

After a while she was joined by two men on flute and drum. She introduced the next song as "Nomad love song/Exile's lullaby" and those were the last words she spoke. She occasionally sang a bit in a tongue unknown to me, but mostly the music remained instrumental and relentlessly hypnotic. I didn't notice the time passing until I stepped outside and it was almost dawn. The song had lasted for about four hours.

The sky was deep blue and clear after the rain. Only a few stars were left in the sky. The peace that is particular to that time filled me and I was glad to be alone with the night and the feeling of dawn approaching. It was a sweet peace that stayed with me as I finally went to sleep with the morning.

In the next few days I asked around about this woman. Everyone had heard something about her, but no one knew much. Her name was the Reverend Egypt. She was new to the city. She was a preacher as well as a singer. She spoke many languages. She came from one of the desert tribes. She had lost her family to the plague. She was a former courtesan. She apparently had oracular abilities and was adept at interpreting dreams.

Everyone I spoke to desired her. I too was intrigued and enamored. The poet had also met her and believed she was currently

45

spending a lot of time at the Gates of Hell.

At my next opportunity, I went looking for her there. This time it was midday, and the cafe had an entirely different look. It could have been a gloomy little place, but someone had put in skylights. One, two, or even three regular skylights would have made it a nice but ordinary place, but almost thirty small square skylights had been installed. At this time of day, the place was filled with columns of light. It was stunning, a suitable frame for the Rev. Egypt.

Playing chess by the wall, hers was an unmistakable presence, covered in a style reminiscent of Eastern women from centuries past. She wore clothing dyed a deep indigo blue with cinnabar stitching on the seams. Her cap and veiling were of one piece that draped around her neck and shoulders, revealing only her eyes. Her long-sleeved top tightened at the wrists and grew gloves that ended at the first joints of her fingers. It covered her torso loosely and tucked into her trousers, which were tight at the hips and covered with pockets and pouches. Her trousers ballooned from her hips, harem style, and tucked into her black leather boots. Her nomad eyes were the color of night and in them was a look seen in those who spent a lot of time in the desert or anyplace without walls: keen, alert, and far-seeing.

I sat and watched her while she played chess. Her eyes were abstract as she focused on the strategies and possibilities laid out before her on the board, but when she glanced up her dark eyes seized me like a falcon. I waited out the game. Her fingers fascinated me as they elegantly and precisely moved her pieces. The game ended in a stalemate, her opponent thanked her and left. She turned her eyes to me again.

"I hear you interpret dreams," I began.

She nodded, her eyes beckoning, her hand with a graceful gesture inviting me to sit down. I had been rehearsing the words in my mind all day, hoping for this opportunity.

"I am stretched out on a pile of rose petals," I blurted out. "The rose petals are alive, moving over me, permeating me with their colors and fragrance. I am watching from outside myself as I have an orgasm that shakes both my body and the rose petals, like a breeze shaking the wheat fields. It looks so lovely that I don't know which is more pleasurable, the sight or the feeling.

"Then I am dressed in a suit and sitting at a typewriter, typing. I look at the paper and words and see I am typing out hieroglyphics. I do not understand their meaning but that does not confuse me nor does it diminish my concentration or my intent. The paper turns into fire made of the same colors as the rose petals and covers my hands. It doesn't burn, instead the soft feeling of my hands melting in the flames orgasms me again and I wake up. "

She looked through me for a moment. She remained quiet long enough to make me nervous. I sat there, waiting, like some awkward schoolgirl. Sitting close to her, I became aware of a lovely fragrance emanating from her, the scent of roses combined with the clean smell of sunlight. This unexpected echo of my dream made me even more nervous. At last she spoke.

"I am walking down a deserted highway. I have a suitcase with me. It is old and battered and I love it. The sun is going down and suddenly there is a city in front of me. I am afraid to enter the city and I turn around, but then I'm in the middle of the city and it's night and I'm surrounded by neon lights. Geisha girls bustle by me in flocks, giggling and pointing at me. I go home. I am five years old and my pants are torn at the knee. I crawl under my bed and find a trap door there. I go through it and I am flying in space. I stretch out my arms and they are miles wide."

Silence again. Then her eyes twinkled at me.

"A dream for a dream."

"But what does my dream mean?" I asked petulantly. I felt like a small child whining, suspicious of trickery.

"Wrong question," she replied. "The question is, what is a dream?"

She got up. She was done with me. I watched her glide away, angry yet envious of her grace and magnetism.

I left the Gates of Hell and walked home, embarrassed and ashamed of what I now saw as an obvious ploy for her attention. Rarely had I had so beautiful or so erotic a dream, so I went running to her with this one, hoping she would perceive me as sensual, attractive, worthy of her interest.

And the hieroglyphics! Of course I would want the Rev. Egypt to take that as a sign that my destiny was intertwined with hers. My face burned. She was no doubt laughing at me.

I hated her and her phony ways.

47

5. Evolution

phoenix   1. Egyptian mythology. A bird that consumed itself after 500 years and rose renewed from its ashes. 2. A person or thing of unsurpassed excellence or beauty; paragon. 3. Female genitalia.

The next day, while walking through the communal areas on my way to the kitchens, I saw several people in the video room watching the Rev. Egypt. I joined them, and later watched the tape several more times. Technology enabled us to see her draped in undulating smoke and her words become pictures. This is what she said:

"I am walking on the water and the bottoms of my feet are covered in fur. I bend over to touch the water with my fingertips and they fall in velvet droplets of midnight blue. I let go and the result is I become a fish and breathe in a different way. Opening my eyes, they become tunnels that lead to a cave filled with the fragrances of frankincense and lust. I banish my heart to the land above because that is where humanity lives and without them my heart would dry up. Now, in the water I cannot live without a heart so I return to land. I open my chest and put my heart back in which bloodies my hands so I wash the bloodie off in the water, watching crimson and midnight blue blend to form iridescent violet. Weary from my activities I lay down beneath a palm tree and through half shut eyes watch birds emerge from my limbs and soar to the clouds. I smell the moisture of an oasis under my body while palm branches, whispering in the breeze, fan me with shade. I feel luxurious in my soft old cotton gown. Looking over the curve of my hip as I lay on my side I decide I am beautiful and need no more than this, and so on until a man stands in front of me at which time I melt into the sand and reconvene by the city's gate. I buy an orange from an old toothless vendor with lechery in his one good eye and pause a moment to get my bearings. I listen to the crowds filling the marketplace. Following the rhythm of coins exchanging hands I begin to dance, a dance in celebration of my hips gliding softly in their allotted movement, gently swaying until all the people are gathered around me and one man, bolder than most, kneels before me, raising my gown and kissing me most respectfully between my legs. His hands hold my hips still after a fashion, though my blood continues to dance. I feel the wetness creeping out of my most holy place like a secret spring in the desert. The man opens his trousers, crying out for me. As he enters me, the voice of the crowd marvels. Through this man I envelop the whole crowd and all the people penetrate me. This is what I was born for: I am the Daughter of Humanity. When the man comes, his sperm joins my blood to become a gold and crimson fish that swims up my spine and leaps out of my mouth, showering the people with blessings. I go among the crowd and ask them who it is they want. Their answers echo in the cavern of my womb: an oracle, that they may behold the Mystery; a Christ saviour, that they may know the Mystery; and a lover, that they may embrace the Mystery. This was the beginning of my ministry."

This tape had recently been shown on the community access station, the first in a projected series of twelve. It was not surprising to hear there would be a demonstration in front of the station. I was curious and went to see what was going on, though I rarely went into the New City.

When I arrived, there were about fifty demonstrators chanting "We are Christians and we care! No more Egypt on the Air!" Signs were carried proclaiming, "Outlaw Blasphemy," "Pornography Is Not Holy,""Whore of Babylon," "Catholics against the Rev. Egypt," and my favorite, "Egypt is Not the Promised Land!"

Watching the demonstrators, I was struck by how dour they looked and wondered why people believed that God appreciated their anger and unhappiness. I sighed, thinking that really it was none of my business. Events like this were not so entertaining after all.

Just as I turned to leave, a face caught my attention. Surrounded by the crowd, his face stood out like no other could for me: Father Jacobson. It had been a long time and it took me a minute to recognize him, but my body had known his immediately. His sign read, "Virgin Mary, Pray For Us."

Everything stood still for a moment. I was shocked to find him in this city, thousands of miles away from where we had last met. When the picket line brought him closer and he saw me, I said hello. He muttered something and stared at me before turning his face away. I had grown up since the last time I saw him, so I wasn't surprised that he didn't recognize me, but I was certain from the way he stared that something in him knew me, knew my scent, knew my aura, the same way I had known him.

Thoughts of him kept me up all night. It's true he had fucked me before I was ready, but we had also shared some wonderful times together. I had loved him in a grand mixture of religious fervor, sexual awakening, and the passion of first love. After all these years, I was able to forgive him his trespasses.

Or was I? The next day I found myself calling all the Catholic churches in the New City to find him. He was now pastor of St. Joseph's Church. I found out when he heard Confessions.

When the appointed afternoon came, I was shaking as I dressed myself. I could not stop to think about it too much: I just went through the motions of garters, stockings, no underwear, dress, shoes, veiled hat. Head to toe in black, except for my crimson garter belt. Silk stockings, silk garters, silk dress; I was trembling inside the embrace of silk.

I ventured again into the flat grey streets of the New City which, as always, seemed stale and boring compared to the kaleidoscope of the Old City. On this day, though, my surroundings only served to make me feel more adventurous by contrast.

I went early and knelt with a rosary in the rear pew, waiting for him to arrive. Watching him enter the confessional, then following, opening the door, kneeling in the dark, I was as frightened and as excited as when I was a child. I was not a child now, though. I was a woman.

When the partition scraped open, I was ready and spoke,"Bless me Father for I have sinned. It has been 23 years since my last confession.

"I ate 18,253 meals without gratitude. I smoked 17,605 cigarettes, which may have shortened my life span by approximately 67 days, 5 hours, and 27 1/2 minutes. It didn't seem like that much time. Maybe someday it will.

"I told 5,921 lies about myself, but they were only little lies and sometimes I didn't know that I was lying. I committed 5 acts of physical violence against my loved ones, 7 acts of physical violence in self defense, allowed myself to be the recipient of 13 acts of physical violence, and learned that in some cases it is not more blessed to give than receive.

"I aborted 7,893 creative ideas. I spoke 19,628 bad words and entertained 15,891 bad thoughts; that is, words and thoughts that judged, criticized, condemned, belittled, or injured myself or others. I wasted countless precious moments in guilt and in fear.

"I also wasted a lot of time holding a grudge against someone I once loved, someone I thought treated me badly. Do you know what I mean, Father? Do you perhaps also waste time, possibly in regret, or worse still, in denial?

"There was a time in my life when I lived for coming to confession, to speak my sins and receive my penance. There was a priest who heard my confession and taught me how to pray. He taught me other things, too. Do you know the sound of my voice, Father Jacobson?"

He didn't respond, and I remained silent for a time, letting the charge between us build. He knew it was me. There is no place that holds silence like a confessional and no environment that amplifies feelings like that dark, private cubicle. I had been unable to keep my hands off myself from the moment I stepped in and the juicy, slurping sounds of my self-pleasuring echoed through the confessional, adding to my excitement. I had been taking my time, both with myself and with what I had to say. Then my control broke.

"I hated you for years. You fucked me before I was ready. I loved you! I trusted you! You hurt me." My voice broke as the tears came, releasing my pain to the confessional. I hadn't expected this, but didn't try to stop it. There was a sweetness about weeping in the dark. When it was over a more reflective mood came upon me.

"Let me confess this to you, Father. For a long time I hated the word "fuck." Some people used it as a mean word, others used it so carelessly it had no meaning at all. I didn't like fucking, either. It reminded me of you. It never felt good, though I kept trying. Then I met a man, a poet, who taught me a secret: the word "fuck" sounds beautiful when you say it wholeheartedly, fucking feels great when you do it wholeheartedly, and life is wonderful when you live it wholeheartedly.

"My problem was never the word "fuck" or the act of fucking. It was fear. Were you scared too, Father? Is that why you did it? Did you need to end it between us? Were you afraid someone would find out? Did you feel guilty about the whole thing? Did it hurt you to not be able to hold back that day or are you just an ass? Don't tell me. I don't really care now. I want to remember the exciting times we had and forget the rest.

"Being with you here in the confessional gets me hotter than anything else. I bet it's the same for you and you got hard as soon as you heard my voice. I bet you're hoping you'll get to fuck me again. Are you wondering what I've learned in the last twenty-three years? Are you wanting to ask me for things you couldn't ask me for when I was ten? Would you like to give me penance and have me climb in there with you?"

He gave no reply to my monologue. I didn't want him to. This was my day. I had complete control and relished the feeling. I felt his cock straining for me, a palpable presence on the other side of the partition.

"What about your penance, Father? I know your thoughts right now are not worthy of a priest hearing Confession. I brought my rosary with me. I could whip you with it but I don't think you deserve a rosary for penance." When I spoke the words rosary and penance I came.

"Bless me Father, for I think your cock would feel really good this time."

I struggled to return to my teasing game.

"But there is still the matter of your penance. Perhaps I should wipe myself off with your robe and make you wear it like that for a week.

"Even better, I will not fuck you today and you will wait for me, not knowing when or if I will come back. Pray, Father. Pray that I stay here long enough to listen to you beg me for it. Get down on your knees. Pray and beg."

I heard him comply and kneel. To me he said only one word, "Please." A litany of passion, repeating this one word, letting his desire fill his voice, begging most beautifully.

I could not hold back, nor did I want to. I stepped into in his portion of the confessional and rubbed my dripping phoenix hard against his mouth. Then I put him back on his chair, sitting on his lap and taking him. The feel of his penis was like no other. It was a grand feeling to take and enjoy what had once been forced on me. The cubicle was small but I managed to squat on his lap, taking his arms and holding them back against the wall.

His eyes were open, adoring me, utterly receptive to me. He kissed my breasts with reverence. He waited until I had had enough and I gave him permission to come. I could tell it was difficult for him to hold back and was impressed with his efforts.

We were both drenched in sweat when he moved to sit me down on his chair and knelt between my legs. Fortunately both of us were small people and so we managed, though barely, to maneuver ourselves within the confessional's confines.

Several times, people entered the confessional and we had to be silent until they assumed no one was there and left. I am normally a noisy lover, and the need for restraint and occasional silence was excruciatingly exciting for me. He balked at what I wanted to do while he heard a confession but I took him in my mouth and he could not refuse me.

When we were done, I kissed Father Jacobson deeply on the mouth. We caressed each other with many sweet words before we parted. Walking out of the church, the sunlight stung my eyes after the darkness of the confessional. I remembered being released from my punishment in the closet and Jesus emerging from the tomb. The darkness had been sweet to me and stepping from the darkness into the light was sweeter still. My satiated body was singing: passion had triumphed over trauma. It was a wonderfully healing experience.

I never went to see Father Jacobson again. Everything we had for each other was expressed in that one afternoon. Anything further would have taken away from the perfection of that meeting.

6. Initiation (inhalation)

inspire   3. To elicit; create. 4. a. To affect, guide, or arouse by divine influence. b. To communicate by divine influence. 5. To inhale (air). 6. Archaic. a. To breathe upon. b. To breathe life into. -intr. 1. To rouse latent energies, ideals, or reverence. [Middle English inspiren, from Old French inspirer, from Latin inspirare, to breathe into.]

Friday was my favorite day of the week. At dawn I'd walk deep into the labyrinth of the market in the heart of the old city, delivering a pack full of fresh herbs to be sold at Paloma's shop. The market would just be waking up, empty of the crowds that would bargain, jostle and shout there later in the day. I'd take the opportunity for a meditative stroll along the cobblestone pathways, enjoying the jumble of bright colors, pungent smells and clashing voices of the market, sometimes stopping for tea with Paloma or one of the other shopkeepers I was getting to know.

Afterwards I'd go to the Turkish baths, located nearby, and step into a haven of women: nubiles, crones, mothers, daughters, and grandmothers of all shapes, colors, and sizes, all languorous and melting in the steam, the heat, and the waters. There were women with breasts that had nourished and nurtured almost a whole tribe of babies, women with breasts whose sole purpose in life was pleasure, and others still who had lost their breasts to the plague. Some woman came there to socialize, others, like me, came to be alone, but all of us came to be taken out of our daily routines and renewed.

Here in the old city we didn't all speak the same language. The murmuring of those I didn't know soothed me, accompanied by the voice of water singing in its own fluid tongue. The melodic sounds seemed to quiet the words that could make themselves so important in my brain. I'd follow the images of women walking through veils of mist and let time slip away. I confess that I love to dream more than I like to think. I suppose that's why I preferred to go to the baths alone, hidden from the world by the the vapors; naked, anonymous, and silent.

The cafe next door to the baths was called the Oxygen Feather. The back of the cafe featured a solarium fed by a grey water system from the baths. Huge, ropy philodendrons and other lush, tropical greenery surrounded a lavish waterfall and pond. All around grew massive timber bamboo. One could recline in areas of carpets and pillows or sit at one of the tables dotted around the solarium. An oxygen bar sat discretely off to the side for anyone who did not feel sufficiently replenished from the atmosphere.

The tall ceilings and archways in the front of the cafe were painted in billowy blues and whites, suggesting clouds and sky, while dolphins and mermaids cavorted in the foaming waters on the lower portions of the walls. The tables were covered in lapis blue mosaics and designs that echoed the walls. I usually went there after the baths for mint tea.

When I heard the Rev. Egypt was giving talks I felt conflicted about attending one. Since she had taken little notice of me, I wanted to dislike her or at least feel indifferent, but the truth was she intrigued me. I resisted the idea of becoming her groupie, disciple or hanger-on, but my desire for her was strong. Emotionally, spiritually, and sexually I desired her. She was a soul magnet.

One Friday I arrived at the Oxygen Feather to find the solarium unusually crowded. The Rev. Egypt was about to make an appearance. Call it fate. My guts floated and my heart raced in nervous anticipation as I squeezed in and found myself a spot on the floor.

She walked in naked except for her veiling. It was disconcerting. I have consistently seen people dressed from the neck down, faces showing. I have frequently seen people naked. The first time I saw the Rev. Egypt was my first time seeing someone with a covered face, and this was the first time I had ever seen someone naked with their head and face hidden. Her indigo veiling covered her face, draped around her neck and hung down her back. Only her eyes were visible, her dark falcon's eyes.

Her body was round, her breasts full, her thighs strong, her neck proud. She had a long scar on one leg, a warrior turned priestess with the proportions of a courtesan. She was too poised to be titillating and too graceful to be merely erotic.

In front of the pond she sank down, sat on her heels, closed her eyes, and began to rock back and forth. I was nervous, squirming as I sat, waiting for her to look at us and say something. She was not behaving in any way I was accustomed to. It was profoundly disturbing.

She just continued to rock, steadily and hypnotically. Rocked until her movement slowed me down and began to speak to me. Rocked, and showed me a mystic lost in ecstasy, immersed in the inhalation and exhalation of the cosmos. Rocked, and became an old man voicing his prayers to his God, aching for His presence and comfort.

Rocked, voicing a woman's grief as she holds a loved one in her arms, watching blood flow useless onto the ground. Rocked, and revealed a lover joined to the beloved in the sweet yielding of passion. Rocked, embodying a young mother soothing her infant to sleep, enchanted by the life that has come through her. Rocked, celebrating the freedom of a woman riding toward the horizon, riding the undulations of camel, woman, heat and desert.

Rocked, and brought my heartbeat into rhythm with hers, teaching me without words, taking me into the myriad hearts of humanity. Rocked, and gave me a glimpse of how to at last enter my own precious heart.

When eventually she spoke with words, this is what she said:

"It can be as simple as this: open and close, back and forth, expand and contract, empty and full, a rhythm your body already knows, the rhythm of breath, heartbeat, lovemaking, life. Remember this and you can know everyone and everything."

She picked up a wide, brass ceremonial bowl, dipped it into the pond, rose and, lifting her veil a little, raised it to her lips, blew on the water it contained, then stretched forward her arms, offering the bowl to us with a classical gesture.

"Cleanliness is next to godliness, they say."

She raised the bowl above her head and poured the water over herself. She stood there, naked, wet and glorious, with laughter and mischief in her eyes.

"So worship me."

Orgasm swept through me as if her fist were opening in my secret place, reaching up to untie the knots in my belly and open a portal to my heart. An explosion in my cells, releasing the center of my being, opening my body, my emotions and my thoughts: I had never felt so alive. In a moment the world had changed and was now filled with a luminosity I had never known before. My heart was breaking open to contain it and the breaking felt sweet beyond imagination. She laughed, silk billowing in the breeze, while the bamboo rustled and I kept on unraveling.

After a time, she spoke again.

"Air is all-pervasive, yet we often deny its presence and disregard its touch. Though we may choose to ignore it, our breath comes to us automatically, unconditionally giving us life. In this sense, the air that surrounds us is the messenger of God.

"We come from a culture that is uncomfortable with intimacy. We like to wear clothes and shit behind closed doors. We like to think of the Supreme Being as residing far away in the heavens rather than permeating our bodies. We also like to forget that the air we breathe is shared with everyone, that it has no regard for our personal boundaries and petty prejudices.

"Breath does not discriminate as it penetrates and fills everyone. When people ask me what my favorite sexual activity is, I tell them it's breathing - I get to do it with everyone all the time. All breath is Holy Breath. It's both Mother and Mother's milk, lover and lover's caress, friend and friend's constancy.

"This Holy Breath is God loving you, giving you life, dancing through the temple of your body. The Holy Spirit was once known as the Holy Breath and considered the feminine aspect of the Christian Trinity. Call it sacrament, call it holy communion, ritual, cosmic lovemaking, survival, the omnipresence of God; the Holy Breath is all this and more. Can you see that breathing can be so much more than a passive, shallow event?" Her voice was soft but carried as if she were whispering in my ear.

"Let your every inhalation be a healing and every exhalation a blessing. Welcome the Holy Breath that embraces you within and without. Each breath is an opportunity. Every inhalation can take you to heaven, every exhalation can release you into the wonder of the present moment, free and unencumbered.

"The Holy Breath holds you all in its loving embrace. You are never really separate or isolated. Your breath, your God, your beloved, your family, your world, your life: it is all the same. Let your breath be full and deep.

"You can separate in thought, but not in breath. Blessed and touched by the Holy Breath, it is an intimacy that we always share, a sacrament of which we continuously partake. Feel the power of the Holy Breath flowing through you and all those around you. There is nowhere it will not go; nourishing us, sustaining us, embracing and loving us, it is truly an ocean of mercy."

She sang,

"O cean of mer cy
O shen of myrrh, see?
mur mur ocean, oh shen mur mur oh myrrh
ommm merci
mur mur ommm shen see ocean of mercy ommm
amen.

Mesmerizing me with her voice of silk and brook, she continued with a litany,

"I am a woman; I transform
I am a man ; I resurrect
I am a prophet; I babble
I am a stranger; I question
I am a sphinx; I riddle
I am an angel; I comfort
when I am a man I orbit like a planet
when I am a planet I nourish like a heart
when I am a heart I embrace like a woman
when I am a woman I speak like a kiss
when I am a kiss I linger like a dream
when I am a dream I blur like a shadow
when I am a shadow I cling like an infant
when I am an infant I am blessed like water
when I am water I permeate like time
when I am time I disperse like air
when I am air I travel like thought
when I am thought I illumine like fire
when I am fire I dance like love
when I am love I am infinite like sky
when I am love I am everything."

As she chanted, I grew increasingly aware of the presence of this Holy Breath of which she was speaking. By this time we were all sprawled out together on the solarium floor and I was laying with my head on someone's lap. I felt his breath in rhythm with my own.

It was as she said: we were not separate from one another. I felt a deep intimacy with everyone, a sensation like sexual union, but more profound and juicy than any I had yet experienced. And I would never stop breathing as long as I lived! This intimacy was continuous, a fact of being alive.

We had been numb to it, but Egypt had brought us back. I burrowed into her aura as if I were nestled in her arms. I floated on a bed of dreams, on pillows of clouds, softer and more innocent than anything I'd ever known. In trust we all lay together, for a while free of fear. That was her gift to us.

When I left there that day it didn't seem necessary to speak with the man upon whose lap I had rested, but that was my first meeting with Baptiste.

Baptiste was almost always with the Rev. Egypt, for it was he who managed the collage she called her ministry. She gave talks at the Oxygen Feather, played music at the Gates of Hell, presented beautifully cryptic performances all over the old city and, to a lesser extent, extended her art into video and tv.

One evening at the Gates of Hell I sat next to Baptiste and he held my hand. I didn't think then about falling in love, I just noticed how comfortable my hand felt in his, an ease I had never experienced before; not with my family, not with my friends and not with any of the people I had called lovers.

I hadn't really noticed Baptiste before that. He was not the kind of man who drew attention to himself. After that night, though, I started to watch him and even went to the studio one day to observe while he directed a music video of one of the Rev. Egypt's songs, a popular song of hers called "Apocalyptia."

"My name is Apocalyptia, spike heels on the tundra
Raised on rattlesnake milk in the
Gardens of Siberia.
Thought I was tough till I contracted malaria
And spent long years weeping in deliria and hysteria.
Then while eating barbed wire I cut open my eye
And discovered my true calling was to be a messiah."

The studio was filled with tribal drummers and the technicians made their staccato hands appear like throngs of butterflies alighting on the Rev. Egypt's robes. Barbed wire took on the appearance of a starry night. The most beautiful shot was one recently completed by the computer graphics team that showed the Rev. Egypt surfing a huge wave, one hand pulling aside her robe to expose her sacred heart à la Jesus Christ, while her other hand was poised in a wish-granting gesture from the Hindu pantheon of divinities.

It was a great party. The drummers played constantly and the entire shoot moved to their festive rhythms. Sound, camera and special effects were all played live under the direction of Baptiste and the inspiration of the Rev. Egypt. I was put to work as an extra pair of hands, mostly moving cable and other unskilled tasks. I thoroughly enjoyed myself.

Baptiste spent a lot of time with the Rev. Egypt and obviously worked comfortably and harmoniously with her. He didn't seem enthralled the way many others were. I admired his composure. As someone who was not always comfortable working with a group (even at the farm I often worked alone), I was fascinated by the ease with which he inconspicuously commanded the situation. The unpretentious Baptiste and the flamboyant Rev. Egypt made an excellent team.

He was nothing the tribes would have ever produced; a tall skinny white guy, sparing in both speech and body language. He had no faux tribal affectations of tattoo or piercing, nor did he wear any jewelry. He was clean shaven and wore glasses. Now that I had noticed him, his simplicity seemed potent, unique and very attractive.

There was one thing about him, though, that sent me into turmoil. He had no right hand. I don't know how it had ever escaped my attention. It made it impossible for me to talk to him for very long or even look at him very much, though I continued to seek out his company. I was somewhat embarrassed around him, certain that no one could miss the fact that my eyes were riveted to his arm. I tried not to stare but couldn't help myself. I wondered if he had known other people who had felt the way I did. A few? Many? None? Could I tell him? How would I tell him? Would he be offended? Shocked? Delighted? I had no experience with this kind of situation. I became obsessed.

Aesthetically, the missing hand gave Baptiste the aura of an outlaw, which contrasted intriguingly with his reserved demeanor. Visually, it was the way his arm ended neatly at the wrist, solid and strong, flesh and bone that was like a cock but not a cock, constantly flaunting itself in public as an erection rarely could, that made me drool whenever I saw him, which was often.

He was at most of the Rev. Egypt's events and in the sensitive atmosphere created by the Holy Breath I felt self-conscious and exposed around him. I was afraid that Baptiste would be offended by my desire, since even I didn't always approve of it. He was such a quiet man. I knew next to nothing about him. What if to him the loss of his hand was an unhealed tragedy? Though I didn't think that was the case, in matters of love and lust my intuition had often proved itself unreliable.

I feared I was objectifying him with my obsession over his arm, but I knew in my heart that it was Baptiste I craved, and that his arm was a wonderfully unusual turn-on about him that would not have been as powerful with someone else.

Meanwhile, people were flocking to Egypt's performances, where she displayed her splendid self as icon, temptress and prophet. Apart from never uncovering her face, she seemed thoroughly uninhibited about revealing herself. She sang, danced, wailed, babbled poetry and whatever else the moment called for.

One of the first performances I saw was called "Mistress of the Kali Yuga." It began with her speaking in darkness while a soft light traversed and illumined sections of her body:

> "When I was a goddess,
> meditating in the shadows of time,
> exquisitely gleaming in solitude,
> I was not crucified,
> though I was violated now and again.
> I went willingly into bondage
> for the sake of love."

The performance culminated with her making love to her body, saying good-bye to her physical life as it was sacrificed on the altar. I had never before thought that public masturbation could be such a poignant act.

Another performance was called "Eve's Kundalini." This was primarily a dance piece. I have seen other people dance with snakes, and for the most part they use their snakes as props and adornments. Egypt moved with her snake as equal partners, slithering hypnotically together in a boneless flexibility.

Though her performances were both visually and aesthetically thrilling, Baptiste told me that Egypt's purpose in everything she did was to infiltrate and saturate people's minds with the idea of the Holy Breath. To this end she dedicated all her art and grace. Her images, sounds, and movements were intended to communicate the

Holy Breath directly at the level of people's instinctive selves, bypassing limiting conceptual programs and belief systems.

She also loved to speak about the Holy Breath and regularly gave talks at the Oxygen Feather. I attended both her talks and performances, but after a while it became difficult for me. When I was partaking of the rarefied atmosphere at one of Egypt's events, sitting next to an attractive person, hearing the voice of Egypt, it was easy to embrace the intimacy of the Holy Breath.

Breathing was not an activity that I could take up or put down according to my mood and environment, however, and at times it tormented me to walk past an old drunk with vomit in his beard or a cross-eyed derelict with a mangy dog and feel the sharing of breath.

Sometimes I berated myself for my fear and the superficiality of my heart. More often, I just wanted to wash my hands of the whole idea. I felt infested by the Rev. Egypt's teachings. I could not get rid of them and I could not just stop breathing, either. It was a dilemma that for a while gave me no rest.

During this time I continued to go hear her speak, not because it gave me pleasure, but because I felt trapped. I wanted to be able to breathe in peace. One day when I attended a meeting at the Oxygen Feather, cursing her in my mind, feeling angry and resentful, she walked amongst the crowd as she spoke and stopped directly in front of me.

Piercing me with her eyes, she asked, "Is your breath mine?" Taking hold of me roughly with her arm around my neck, she raised me from my chair, and lifted her veil just enough to kiss me. She cupped her hand around my crotch and I felt my menstrual blood at that moment begin to flow. She withdrew her hand and raised her stained palm, showing it to me with an ancient and holy gesture of openness and peace. The smell of my blood excited me. How had it crossed the barrier of my clothing? She rubbed her bloody palm on my cheek, then walked away.

I felt dizzy and about to lose my balance, so I quickly sat down again. I touched my cheek and felt my blood. I looked up at her. She was standing at her usual place at the waterfall as if she had never moved. The people around me were watching her as if nothing had happened. I touched my cheek again. There was nothing there. Her words were barely audible to me through the roaring sound inside my head.

"Demolish the walls in your mind, the barriers around your heart. Know the clear sky of freedom. Though you have looked into the eyes of your companions a thousand times, they are not as they were yesterday. Do not miss the wonder that awaits you now.

"Be like the wanderer who sleeps every night in a new place on the earth, who speaks little and misses nothing. There is a new you every day, and a new world around you. If you do not experience this, that does not mean it is not true; it only means you have blind-folded your heart with lies.

"You have all closed down your senses, choosing to live the narrowest of visions. You have been taught not to touch, not to know, and to judge only by appearances. You put yourselves to sleep for the sake of love, both the giving and the receiving of it. I ask you now to awaken for the same reason. Do not be afraid. Open your senses, open your heart. I am calling out to you.

"Leave the mausoleum that you live in, the tomb you call your life, the necropolis you call your world. Everything you see is dead because you are frozen in time, viewing your life through screens of the past. You work so hard to keep life away. It's like holding back a tidal wave. No wonder you are so weary. Give it up. Let life in."

The walls around my memory tumbled and I remembered being a child, touching the war, living in confusion, bleeding for my father's pain and seeking serenity from a sky whose thoughts were clouds. I remembered falling asleep, my life before I went to sleep and how much I had craved a person such as the one who now stood before me.

As my childhood memories were revealed to me, I understood my fear of the Holy Breath. My openness as a child had drenched me in the bloodbath of war. Seeing my past clearly, I knew that to accept the Holy Breath completely would not send me back into the war as I had unconsciously feared. The reverse was true. The Holy Breath was the healer that would finally end the war.

One day before Egypt spoke, I had the opportunity to ask her about her clothing. I wondered why she would conceal herself this way at a time when women in other parts of the world were strug-gling to be free of the confinement of the veil.

She replied, "No one has imposed this on me. I wear it freely, to celebrate the Mystery. To do something freely is a different matter entirely, is it not?"

I agreed.

"It also makes it easy for me to disguise myself," she chuckled.

"I have one other question for you," I continued. "What is a dream?" She laughed again. "Sometimes reality; sometimes poetry; sometimes destiny; sometimes a mirage."

Then she glided off to speak, leaving me unsure whether to laugh or pout. I wanted her to talk to me as if I were a friend, not just another person in her audience. My personal opinion was that she needed the veil. It could keep her remote and mysterious while she played a role of such intimacy with so many strangers. I wished she would confide in me.

7. Purification (exhalation)

"Do not be conformed to this world, but be transformed by the renewing of your mind." (Romans 12:2)

It was not yet spring when my father arrived unexpectedly. He looked exhausted and spoke little, as if his pilgrimage to me had drained his reserves. I was surprised to see how much he had aged in the few years since I had last seen him.

That evening we sat together on the roof, sharing a small meal and watching the sunset. Wispy clouds of lavender and peach filled the sky with peace as the day gently gave way to night. My father was so still, so absorbed, that I was startled when he spoke.

"I'm tired."

His voice struck me with its frailty even as it reverberated through the air and filled the twilight around us. A calm statement. I realized he was dying.

I turned to him, wanting to speak and indulge in a marathon of emotions. I wanted us to tell each other our stories and perhaps finally know this man who had fathered me and have him know me. Then I knew, looking at him, that he would not allow it. It didn't matter. All that had gone before was irrelevant. What mattered was his presence now. What mattered was that he had come to me and I had welcomed him. What mattered was the richness of the silence between us.

I led him down to the spare room. The wooden chair and low bed reached out to hold him, the soft blue blanket and feather pillow waited to receive him, the open window brought the sky to him as a gift while the the walls stood tall to protect and enclose him. Was it his dying that made his presence fill the room, that made everything appear so alive?

He sank onto the bed, appearing almost weightless, floating in the soft embrace of the blankets and the strong embrace of the wood. I offered to help him undress but he waved me away with a slight but impatient gesture of his hand.

"I want to sleep,"he said, and closed his eyes, dismissing me.

I reached over and touched his cheek, a little surprised by the depths of my tenderness. His hand covered mine for a moment and he sighed but did not open his eyes. When his hand released mine the magic faded. He was just an old man resting in a poor room.

He seemed to fall asleep immediately. I sat down on the chair and looked out the window for a while, not wanting to leave him even if he didn't know I was there. After a while, the chair was too far away, so I moved it closer. That was comfortable for a while, but then it also felt too far away. Finally I laid down on the bed with him, curled around him spoon fashion, and breathed with him. He was my father. No one else could ever be that.

I didn't realize I had fallen asleep until I woke up, holding only his empty body. I had a vague memory of a dream in which my father and I were walking down a path in the desert, hand in hand. We had been having an important conversation, but I remembered none of it. It was still dark as I held him, grateful that his passing had been so gentle and that those last hours had been spent with me.

I went to the kitchen to get some water and dried fruit, then to my room for an extra sweater and my good shoes, then back to my father's room. Fortunately the room he had been in was on the ground floor. I brought one of the wheelbarrows in from the shed, wrapped him in the blankets he lay on and rolled him into our wheelbarrow. I added a shovel, left a note for the others, covered my head, and started walking west, toward the desert.

The sun was fully risen by the time I reached the city gate. This one was called the Guardian's Gate. To either side the Plague Wall extended northward and southward until it met with the ancient stone gates and walls that surrounded the other half of the city.

Embedded in the gate and wall were parts of bodies: masks of faces, arms reaching out, some to both sides of the wall, some with torsos. The path of the wall itself twisted and bent, sometimes growing archways, ceilings, chambers and grottos, in such a way that it seemed almost natural when a leg emerged or a hand beckoned or a face watched with a silent plea. They all had an eerie eloquence to them.

It was rumored that many of them were actual plague victims who had been covered in plaster and buried within the wall. I believe it to be true. The artist responsible for the wall, Edison Spark, had himself died of the plague. During the two years that it took to complete the wall, many people suffering from the plague had joined him and worked with him. That they would have chosen to be part of the wall after their death seemed right and fitting to me.

Pressing my forehead against the wall, I spoke to the spirits of the builders inside. I asked them to help me understand death and, in asking, became aware of my pitiful ignorance of both death and life. I remained there for an hour or two, feeling comforted and protected. When I stepped away, I experienced a curious tingling sensation in the part of my forehead some call the third eye.

The fig tree outside the gate was barren of fruit but the fountain carried water. I drank some and lingered for a while. It was difficult to leave the comfort of the Guardian's Gate, but it was time to take my father into the desert.

It was sunset three days later when I buried my father. I covered him with dirt and saw his body swallowed up by the earth. When I was done with my work I sat down on my blanket and called forth my memories.

I had known so little about him. He had been a sad, bitter, beaten-down man who did most of his speaking through his paintings. They were largely made up of ruins and shadows and I think that's where his spirit lived, even while he continued to meet the physical demands of day-to-day life.

I wondered what had broken his heart so utterly, whether it was the people he lost to the plague, his unhappy marriage, or something else of which I had no knowledge. I remembered him as a fragile man, bewildered by the world around him, unable to find happiness for himself. I hoped he was happier now.

I lay face down on my blanket with my arms open wide, my father's body below me, our bodies separated by a few feet of earth and the whole mystery of life and death. Embracing my father through the earth, I wept my loss, my loneliness, and my love. Eventually I exhausted myself and just lay there, my cheek pressed against the ground.

With my eyes closed I saw my father. He was laid out on a small boat filled with flowers, sailing on a calm sea toward the sun that was no longer visible to me, trailing flowers as he sailed along the path of golden sunlight, gliding on opalescent waters fed by my tears. Watching the stars come out one by one, each was a memory of a spark of love shared with my father. There were more than I would have expected, and I knew his love then as I had never known it while he was alive.

That night I dreamed of the tribal families I had known as a girl. Their music was as compelling as I remembered and I threw myself into the dance with the same abandon I had known then. Looking around at faces, I saw that some were dead and some were alive. People crowded around me. They wanted me to know their names.

They all told me their names and I remembered them. I climbed up into a tree, a tree with large branches but no leaves. People were clustered in the branches singing. I climbed into the tree and carved all of their names into the wood. Then I pushed off hard with my feet from one of the branches, gliding, dancing, and spinning in the air. All around me was laughter and merry-making. I was laughing, too, as I danced in the air.

I saw my father attempting to come toward me, but his legs were paralyzed. He dragged himself along through the dust, then stopped and reached out to me with his arms. My initial response was to cringe, fearful of his trying to stop me. Then I realized that all his pain and effort was for wanting to join me, to dance with me. It was our combined fear that was paralyzing him.

I picked him up while his body shrank to fit into my embrace. I danced and twirled with him in my arms, our hearts flying to the music, to the night sky, to the stars. We rose together in the sky and, suspended like a twin star, shared the joy that we had always wanted together.

When I awoke, the echo of a flute carried through the still night air. There was a healing on me. I lay quietly, covered by the dark and by the warmth of my blanket. After a time I became aware of a man standing nearby, seemingly waiting for me. Still partially in the dream world, it made sense to trust him, to stand up and follow him. We walked side by side in the light of the setting moon, along a steep but wide path. We followed its switchbacks to the top of the mountain, which we reached just as the sun appeared over the horizon.

The desert mountains, flowing sea-like in subtle undulations, were serenely majestic in their subdued palette of oranges, ochres and yellows. There was no denying the heart and hand of the Creatrix in the sight before my eyes, in the vast waves of rippling desert, in the stillness of the dawn, in the purity of this high place.

My vision was transformed and I was able to see the sands shifting and changing while simultaneously viewing the grand panorama. My mind slowed down and stopped interpreting. I was able to truly see for perhaps the first time in my life. My eyes beheld the expanse before me in a pure sensory communication.

It all touched me through my open eyes: the movement of the sands, the illumination of the dawn as it played with the sinuous shapes of the dunes, the shadows that never really stood still, continuously making their way across the mountains in a slow motion caress, the insects, snakes, and scorpions, the decay that had once lived and now nourished other life, the spaciousness of the sky communing with the spaciousness of the hot, open, flowing desert wilderness, and weaving through it all like the play of light and shadow, the play of life and death that together creates and re-creates the earth. I understood that Creation is the language of God, that this desert dawn, like my father's life and death, was God's poetry and that I, standing there with a stranger, was part of God's poem.

Spontaneously, my hand reached out and took his. We didn't turn to one another but his hand accepted mine. Our hearts were in communion until I started to think about the perverse, petty, egocentric habits of humanity, myself included. I knew that the grace I had been feeling was not meant to be an unusual event and yet in my world it was a rare occurrence.

Self-conscious, I dropped my hand, feeling regret, guilt, and shame. I learned once again the power of those emotions as the spell was broken and the holy moment receded. Looking out over the mountains, I was no longer a part of them. I had removed myself. It saddened me that I was unable to remain in a state of grace and had become separate again. The stranger spoke to me for the first time.

"Behind us are steps that lead down the mountain to the monastery. You can easily find your way from there."

I turned and looked at him. I saw blue eyes, the kind washed pale from long spells of silence and open country, weathered skin, baggy clothes, battered hat; an old desert man. I looked into his welcoming eyes and was drawn in, melting into an echo of my recent experience and along with it a forgiveness and a healing. This morning had been a step in my evolution and would always be a part of my heart. Then an image of Baptiste came to me. I knew that I was in love with him, that he returned my love, and that this, too, was God's poetry. It was time to go home.

I found the steps carved into the rock of the mountain and walked slowly down, contemplating the work and the devotion that had made them, the sweat and the footsteps that had worn and smoothed them. I passed the monastery with indifference and headed east to where the dunes of the desert met the waves of the sea.

Following the sea northward, I swam daily, especially at twilight when the calm sea would turn lavender with the setting sun. The water was a liquid gem, a milky opal in which I immersed myself. The mountains on the other side of the sea were also gem-like and magical in that light and looked close enough to swim to. I never attempted it because the mountains belonged to another country and there was no peace between our borders. The mountains themselves did not share this problem, harmonizing with both the sea and the dunes on the other side to create a hint of a shadow of a glimpse of a memory of paradise. I cherish my memories of what filled my eyes in those days. Perhaps it is true that humanity could not bear to gaze upon the full glory of God. Perhaps that is why we continue to destroy God's glory as it is reflected in nature. We don't like to be reminded of our limitations.

Eventually I had to leave the sea and put myself on the road to the city. As was our custom after the burial of a loved one, I crawled on my hands and knees and by the time the city came into view, rising in the heat like an apparition, it was as if more than one thousand days had passed. I arrived at the city gates as empty as the wheelbarrow I had left to decay in the desert and spent most of the day sitting there, drinking occasionally from the fountain, looking out over where I had been. I was not eager to enter the city with all of its walls and ceilings and people. I didn't want to take on my persona again, to speak and interact. I wanted to remain like this, empty and alone.

After a while, I walked along the wall, studying the faces, the bodies emerging from the wall, passing the occasional surveillance camera discretely placed by those whose business it is to know who goes where. I followed the wall its entire length, walking slowly and exploring its textures with my hands. I wanted to know every inch of it. Occasionally I passed papers tucked into a hand or a mouth, prayers perhaps, or poems. I did not disturb them. It didn't seem right to.

When I finally said good-bye to the wall it was to find Baptiste.

Baptiste was home when I arrived. He let me in and served me tea. I said not a word to him and he responded in kind. He watched me closely and eventually the silence between us became taut and filled with questions. I put my head in my hands and hid my eyes. Vision followed my voice into its retreat. I was unable to speak even now when I wanted to, and unable to look at the questioning in Baptiste's eyes. He waited for a while, but finally asked me why I had come and what was the matter.

"I don't want to see the walls. This house is closing in on me," I rasped. My voice, out of practice, formed words with difficulty. "I don't know how to talk, but I wanted to talk to you. I wanted to tell you I love you but right now my heart is empty, everything is empty. I don't know why I am here."

Baptiste got up and walked away. I didn't look to see where he was going or what he was doing. I wondered if he had ever heard a declaration of love delivered with so little passion. Then I sparked inside for a moment. It was the first time love had been mentioned between us. I knew that to say it had been enough. I could trust Baptiste to emerge me.

He returned and stood behind me. His hand removed mine from my face and replaced them with a soft blindfold which he tied with his hand and his teeth. He picked me up in his arms and carried me for a while, just walking me around. My ear rested on his chest and his heartbeat comforted me. Free of sight, I focused on the sound and rhythm of his body: his breath, his heartbeat, his footsteps.

Gently he put me down and walked away. When he returned, he tore off my clothes, which were grimy and dusty from my time in the desert. It was not the move of a lover; it was more efficient than that. The sound of the tearing cloth announced the end of my desert sojourn and my farewell to my father, bringing me into the present, receptive behind my blindfold to what awaited me here in Baptiste's house.

He picked me up again. He had removed his clothes also and the touch of his flesh was electrifying. He carried me into another room, where I felt steam on my body. He brought me into a large communal tub and laid me down in the water with his arm under my neck and his hand under my sacrum, floating me in the water. He massaged me and stretched me some. When he scooped me up and cradled me in the water, in his arms, I melted into him. His flesh was home.

After taking me out of the bath and drying me thoroughly, he kissed me, not on my lips but on my cheek. The blindfold came off to make room for his lips as they traveled over my cheeks, my eyes, my ears, my forehead, the top of my head, my eyebrows and eyelashes, all over my face before arriving at my lips and then exploring my lips with the same thorough curiosity before opening them to greet my tongue and teeth and saliva and draw out a joysound from the depths of my throat.

Later my eyes would drink of him the way his lips drank of me, but for now my eyes stayed closed, immersed in the touch of the mouth that spoke the soul of Baptiste, the mouth that poured forth an ocean of kisses: elusive butterfly kisses, gentle flower petal kisses, wild and adventurous kisses, greedy devouring kisses, deep, exuberant kisses, hot rapturous kisses, the language of his spirit. His kisses covered the entire mantle of my flesh and when he reached my other mouth, it was longing to kiss him, too. My nether mouth was shameless in its passion, drooling, sighing, panting, quivering, begging; reaching out to him, deliriously open and ready, eager to embrace him and draw him deep into the inner sanctum, the moist, pulsating grotto, my mysterious place.

Spiritually speaking, Baptiste went for the jugular: stripping me down to my primal pulse, stripping me completely naked for the first time in my life. Filling me in the way I had both desired and feared, his arm was a lightning bolt annihilating all my personal boundaries, exploding me into multi-dimensional fragments of fire and light; his arm strong with flesh and bone and sinew, strong with purpose, strong with the longing of his exiled hand.

I surrendered my heart on the altar of his body. Making love with him was a dream of his cock penetrating me as a warrior, drawing me onto a spirited horse that rode us away into distant lands, filled with dreams and visions of paradise, our breath one our hearts one our sprits one. I embraced him with all of my heart, the Mystery devoured us, and after that I did not sleep alone.

8. Celebration

orgy   A secret rite in the cults of Demeter, Dionysus, or other Greek or Mediterranean deities, typically involving frenzied singing, dancing, drinking, and sexual activity. (Greek, from orgia, secret rites)

That summer was a powerful time for me, influenced by the triple catalyst of my father's death, the teachings of the Rev. Egypt, and my love affair with Baptiste. I was working hard, feeling strong and open in the heat.

I was blossoming under the care of Baptiste, who was delighted that I was so turned on by his arm. He tantalized me by not revealing the truth of how he lost his hand. When we lay contentedly together after lovemaking, he would tell me stories of border skirmishes, of escapes on horseback, of defying injustice, of maverick adventures, of magic encounters; endless tales of how his hand had left him or had been taken away from him.

He was an excellent storyteller and his imagination knew no bounds. His stories were by turns sad, painful, frightening, exhilarating, funny, sexy, and romantic. Though I didn't find out the truth about his hand from them, I learned a lot about Baptiste's internal geography and cherished his company more every day.

We experimented with each others bodies, as young lovers are wont to do. It fascinated me to love his forearm with my mouth during sexual union. Since I thought of it as another cock, it was an unusual pleasure to not have to protect it from my teeth: on the contrary, their strength and appetite were welcome.

The fierce aspect of my passion collected in my mouth, sucking, gnawing and chewing Baptiste's forearm, a tigress seated upon the lotus flower that received him with utter tenderness and surrender. Kali and Parvati, devouring above and yielding below, fire issuing from my mouth and flowing water from my nether mouth: the I Ching would call me a goddess hexagram. Though it was not the only pleasure we devised with Baptiste's attributes, it was psychically the most unusual.

The Rev. Egypt took a break from all her public activities except for talks at the Oxygen Feather, focusing the rest of her time on writing a book of her teachings. She could leave no communication medium untouched. It gave Baptiste more free time and, since the farm was busy, Baptiste easily became part of the group. We worked side by side and our relationship as friends and workmates grew alongside our love relationship. Each fed the other and life was sweet.

We began work early to avoid the midday heat. The pre-dawn silence was something we both enjoyed and, as we grew accustomed to working together, we often fasted from speech until the sun rose some two hours into our day. The heat of the afternoon was sleep time. The hours of sunset, twilight and evening found us exploring the world and each other with a second sleep time between midnight and when our work day began. Some evenings we went to see the Rev. Egypt, some were spent singing and dancing with the others on the farm and some we kept to ourselves.

My infatuation with Baptiste's one-handedness changed the way I felt about myself and others. I became enamored of my own scars. Shedding the need to conceal what I had formerly considered unacceptable or damaged aspects of my body and psyche, I was able to enjoy a spontaneity in our love that left me delirious, free of self-consciousness and background anxiety. I sought out similar aspects in others, the orphaned and disowned qualities, abandoned but alive under the surface. This seeking made my world even richer. When I told Baptiste of this, he confessed that losing his hand had affected him the same way.

One particularly juicy gift for me was the complete release of inhibition during my menstrual flow, which had always been a passionate time for me. I reveled in my menstrual blood, thrilled to have a lover who was willing not only to enjoy it but exalt it. On occasion I revisited the sensual play of adolescence and turned Baptiste and me into tribal warriors, both of us decorated with my blood. Baptiste worshiped my blood and the power of my desire, receiving me as if I were the goddess Kali. Some say that women naturally take on some of Kali's qualities during the time of their menstruation. Since Kali represents woman, sex, and lust all elevated to their transcendental expressions, I was happy to embrace that philosophy.

Kali is naked and wanted my mind naked, free of selfishness, hypocrisy, and self-doubt. She wanted me spontaneous, deeply in touch with my sexuality and primordial self. She wanted desire fulfilled and illusion destroyed. I liked Kali very much. The fearless passion she wanted from me seemed much more fulfilling and true to my heart than the repressive love and/or fear that God the Father had required of me in exchange for my passport to His Heaven.

Still, I could not completely turn away from my religious upbringing and at times wondered how it might all fit together. This time is called the Kali Yuga, or Age of Kali. It is also known in the

West as the time of the second coming of Christ. Could there be any relationship? For the most part though, I was busy engaging in pagan love.

Living on the farm naturally turned our lovemaking in the direction of nature worship. We coupled in all the fields to promote a bountiful harvest. My favorite was the sunflower field, where we danced and made love like two flowers standing side by side. The sunflowers felt like special friends and we visited them often, innocent and playful in the pleasures of our lovemaking.

On one visit to the aroma gardens we picked rose petals and covered a blanket with them. Reclining among them in luxury, we spent a long time in oral play, reveling in our intimate fragrances. We showered each other with rose petals and jasmine flowers, then lay together spoon fashion, our bodies quietly joined, watching the moon travel the sky.

The warm night air encircled us, filled with the scents of jasmine, rose, lavender and rockrose. My blood flowed in harmony with the tides and my breath moved in rhythm with Baptiste's. The aroma garden quickly became our favorite spot for gentle times of sexual communion. We were greedy with the place, but people were kind and didn't mention it.

In our more vigorous moods, we wandered all over, chasing each other through the fields, fucking on top of the city walls. Whenever a fleeting, semi-public opportunity arose, I rode Baptiste's forearm between my thighs in a game we dubbed "Father Jacobson's Ride." Whatever my mood, this never failed to please.

The approach of the harvest moon initiated a great deal of activity around the farm, for the night of its fullness was devoted to celebration in gratitude for the bounty of life and in honor of the cycles of nature. The kitchens bustled with preparations of delicacies, the fields hummed with harvest, and we were all energized with anticipation.

The evening of the festival Baptiste and I harvested melons from our patch. Everyone who worked on the farm had their own patch, in which they grew treats for the collective. Baptiste, being temporary, shared mine. Several people were growing melons, but the consensus was that ours were the best.

We stayed to watch the sunset from a hilltop. Returning home, we came over another hill and directly in front of us rose the moon, so big and red I didn't recognize it. It looked as if it would collide with us, such was its size and the illusion of the clear sky. The sight of it filled us with reverence.

By the time we joined the others in preparing the food and tables, the moon hung bold and golden in the sky, looking like our familiar friend again. Baptiste had the knack for fires and started the cook fire and the bonfire with one match. I had no such skill and was always impressed with his one-handed dexterity. As was the custom, we had all come wearing old clothes. When the bonfire was going strong we threw our clothes in and danced naked around the fire.

The Rev. Egypt was one of the drummers that night. She was the only one clothed, dressed in her all-concealing garments, veiled in mystery and grace. Sitting back from the fire with the drummers, she alone blended into the night, while the other drummers gleamed with sweat, reflecting the firelight on their skin.

Someone brought out a wooden spool. The disks, some eight feet across, were cut off. About ten or fifteen people held each one aloft. Here was center stage for the braver dancers. Baptiste and I claimed one apiece. It was hard at first to balance and stand, much less dance. The people holding them up were careening about, hardly keeping them steady, which was part of the challenge.

Amid much laughter and encouragement and a couple of falls, we got the hang of it and grew bold, shaking and stomping and jumping on to each other's platforms when our bearers brought them close. For our grand finale we jumped recklessly onto each other's platforms, exchanging, then turning to do it again until we dove for each other in mid-air, landing tangled and sweaty in the arms of the kind souls who reached out to cushion our fall.

We relinquished the spotlight and gave others a chance, taking our turn as stage bearers. The dancing was passionate, but carrying the platform was no less so, with our naked bodies sandwiched together and the firelight playing on our laughing faces.

At some point we took a break for food and drink. My head rested on Baptiste's lap while he fed me a pomegranate and the poet massaged my legs. Egypt got up and danced alone in the firelight. Her feet drummed the earth and her body undulated like the wheat fields. Many people were by then in various stages of multiple lovemaking. (It was not a night for coupling. It was a night for celebrating together.)

94

At first it was impossible to believe that she really did what I saw: as she danced, she stepped right into the bonfire. I saw her clothes burning, and then she was dancing naked, exalted, in the fire. Her supple body partnered the flames, moving within the fire as if it were no different than air. Diffused by some trick of the firelight, her face was neither concealed nor revealed.

My eyes did not blink or leave the spot. She faded inside the fire and disappeared. When she rematerialized, faintly visible, imprinted on the fire like a thought or a dream of a woman, her body was as fluid and as radiant as the flames she danced within. She was light incarnate, melding with the pure light of the fire. I watched her grow more solid, my eyes riveted, so miraculous was the sight. I did not see her leave nor did I see her disappear again, and yet after a time she was gone.

I remained sitting by the fire. Though I enjoyed the sounds of pleasure around me, I was not aroused that night. I preferred to keep company with my thoughts and the fire.

There was a heaviness within my mind, perhaps I could call it my personal collection of pain and fear, memories and beliefs that kept me from believing what I had seen, even though something deep within me rejoiced and knew exactly what I had witnessed: Egypt had melted into the fire, abandoned herself to it, and made love with an elemental power.

Something in me ached for that, too; not just to make love near the sunflowers, but to make love with the sunflowers, not just to throw my clothes into the fire, but to cast my soul into its embrace. How could that happen?

I let my pain rest and focused on the sweetness of my desire. Truly the present moment was the key to all fulfillment. The fire whispered to me that it would welcome me when my time came. I felt its heat and moved back, a little frightened. I laughed at myself: I wanted to abandon myself, but only on my terms. Such was the contradiction of my desire.

I noticed Baptiste sitting nearby, also absorbed in his own revery. We were in accord with each other and did not intrude upon each other's silence, nor did the other's presence distract us from our personal meditations. When dawn came, I noticed a gold charm from Egypt's necklace sitting in the embers of the fire. I fished it out and kept it.

The next evening Egypt invited us to supper. There were a dozen of us there altogether, including Baptiste, the poet, and me. The atmosphere was harmonious but subdued after the festivities of the night before, with a touch of magic lingering from Egypt's transfiguration. Those of us who had witnessed it had spoken of it in whispers that morning, but it was not mentioned here.

We met on the rooftop deck, where Egypt had placed a large table, a few couches and some potted palms. We had a view of the old city, the walls, the gates and the desert beyond. It was a stunning yet peaceful sight, especially in the lingering twilight of Indian summer. The food was simple and delicious, as was Egypt's taste. We helped ourselves from large platters of freshly baked bread and dried fish, followed by dates, pomegranates, figs and sweet mint tea.

There was not a lot of conversation and I for one was content to gaze at the expanse below, my thoughts meandering in a perhaps baby-like way, something like, "My life. I love it. This warm breeze feels so good on my skin. Baptiste looks so fine in this light. I would like to make love with him. Egypt is so alluring. She is truly a goddess. This food is delicious. I'm so lucky. Everyone here is so wonderful. The sky is so blue. The desert goes on forever. I love my life."

Egypt had my attention immediately when she was ready for it. She looked around at all of us, taking her time. When she spoke, the words drifted from her mouth like rose petals. She was the most gentle person I had ever known, and the most beautiful, though I had never seen her face.

"Thank you for joining me on such a lovely evening," she began. "Food is always more delicious when shared."

She raised a large crystal goblet. "Listen," she said, and poured water into it.

"Even the sound of water has the power to restore the spirit. Water sings the rhythm of life, gives flexibility to the tall bamboo and causes the desert wildflowers to bloom. It purifies us and renews us when we immerse ourselves in it and gives us life when we drink of it. Our bodies are made up in large part of water. Without the nourishment of water, one cannot live. Love is like water."

She added wine to the cup.

"Wine is the wild joy of life, a cup filled with the treasures of celebration and passion: spontaneous magic, laughter without reason, uninhibited ecstasy, reckless abandon, dancing, revelry, delight. Passion banishes fear, warms cold nights and cold hearts. Love is indeed like wine and God is indeed love. "

She held up the goblet.

"Water and wine are joined together in this cup. Let it be so with your love. If you drink only of passion, you may find that peace eludes you, leaving you disillusioned and bitter. If you drink only of sustenance, life may be little better than existence, never knowing divine intoxication. When you drink the two in one cup, water becomes more than water and wine more than wine. Let this elixir awaken and nurture your deepest and most beautiful desires.

"Share this cup with me now, my friends, and share this cup often in honor of all that we have shared."

She lifted her veil only enough to drink, then passed the cup around. Fascinated, I watched the cup move from hand to hand and mouth to mouth. When I drank, I tasted the truth of what she said: intoxication and sustenance.

Looking over at Egypt, I loved her, for she was not unlike the cup to me. She caught my glance and the cup held to my lips felt for a moment like the secret cup between her legs. She held my gaze, her eyes joining the breeze in its caress.

Passing the cup to the poet, I felt aroused in a heady, languorous way. Life itself was loving me and there was no part of me untouched. It dawned on me that God is Life, that all of humanity is Life's lover and it is our joy and purpose to receive this love.

My body was heavy with a delicious weight. The embrace of gravity holding me close to the earth, the air filling my lungs with the Holy Breath, the heat in the air on my skin, the beauty of my companions and the desert beyond kissing my eyes: Life was penetrating me in a multitude of delightful ways.

The others moved in an intricate dance of harmony; it was much later that I identified the dance as their leaving and going home. At some point Egypt brought a thick blanket out onto the roof for me. I lay on it under the stars, gravity pressing my back to the earth, penetrating me with its power, immobilizing me in its embrace. All my life gravity had been making love to me and I had been oblivious, like someone in a coma. This night was filled with all the sweetness and ardor that a lover feels at the return of one who has been long absent.

Swooning and coming, I drank deeply of this sweetness even as I was overcome and the thought came to me that this was simply the awareness of being alive, without censor or inhibition. Clinging to it and milking it with all the power of my sex, I surrendered to gravity's might and was awestruck when it playfully let me go, flinging me into a weightless, boundless expanse. My body was vast and my body was freedom. Light seemed to emanate from my every cell, illuminating the heavens.

When the sun rose in golden splendor, Egypt came up to the roof and shared another cup with me. It was difficult for me to drink because I could not stop laughing. She gave me a hug that brought me back to earth and fed me some figs.

In a state of rapture I went home to join the continuing harvest.

9. Crucifixion

"Whoever does not love abides in death." (1 John 3:14)

I am shouting with a loud voice until the earth starts to shake , so I stop but the shouting continues to come out of me even though my mouth is shut. I put my hands over my mouth, then around my throat, but I cannot stop. I am riding lava out of a volcano, surfing on red lava, so bright, like blood, and I realize it is the blood of my mother and I am being born. I look up to her face but it is the face of my beloved, not my mother. What is she doing here? I want to sleep. My eyes are heavy. I want her to leave me alone, but she comes closer to me. She wants me to get up. She is insistent. She speaks to me, but I can hear only static coming from her mouth.

I wake up and realize that I have been Baptiste in my dream. I am laying next to him. I want to rouse him. I do not want to fail. I catch that thought. Fail what? What does that mean? I am afraid, unsure of where I am. I wake up again, alone in my room. I lay there for some time, looking at the ceiling, confused.

The emotional tone of this dream disturbed me since I had been happily living in the afterglow of the harvest celebrations for weeks. I put my anxiety aside. Baptiste and I were going to a party in the New City, given by a former lover of his, Catseye Kamikaze.

I rarely went to the New City. To me it was a soulless grid, like every other city I had been in, full of bad air, polluted emotions, toxic thoughts and harmful actions. Any time I entered it, I was proud that the Old City flourished like a fertile oasis so close by. The people living in the New City thought of us as retro-hicks, full of nostalgia and denial, but I didn't mind. Perhaps I was growing superstitious. I was certain that the gates and walls of the Old City protected us, that the labyrinth of its streets purified our minds, that the farm nourished the air, and that the presence of the Rev. Egypt was a continual blessing.

When we arrived that evening, the place was arranged like a fantasy of an Eastern brothel. Oriental carpets covered the floors, which were dotted with areas of large pillows, divans, and small tables holding candles, opium and Turkish delight. Musicians and dancing girls wandered about entertaining, while bare-chested houseboys fanned the guests and lit their opium pipes. The overall effect was lush and decadent.

Catseye circulated in sheer, voluminous harem pants and

nothing else, presiding over the spectacle. She was a striking woman with coloring straight out of an old British folk ballad. Her blood red lips beckoned and her long, thick, straight hair was jet-black. Her skin, the whitest I'd ever seen, was pale and translucent; one could see the delicate filigree of her veins. She had two lovers following respectfully behind her. It was partly submission, but I suspected it was equally for the pleasure of watching the undulations of her round, fleshy ass.

Catseye was also a farmer of sorts. She cultivated narcotic producing plants within the controlled environment of her greenhouse and grew fields of opium poppies at some hidden location outside the city. I believe she had her houseboys doing all the work. It seemed unlikely that she ever went out into the sunlight or got her hands dirty

Despite my recent experiences, I was paralyzed by the sight of her. She was an orchid; I was a kitchen herb. She was exotic; I was common. The knowledge that Catseye had been Baptiste's lover drew out all my deep insecurities. I felt like a fool and tried to hide it. I was jealous and sought to deny it.

I was clearly out of my element. I felt awkward and clumsy while self-assured predators drifted by me through clouds of opium smoke. Though I rarely took drugs, the sweet smell was seductive, hanging in the air like honey mixed with semen. I remembered entering a room, a long time ago, after a woman had fucked forty-nine men in a row. This place reminded me of that room.

I didn't like it then, and I didn't like it any better this time. The atmosphere was just too thick for me. I felt uncomfortable with my lack of sophisticated sexuality. Even the houseboys seemed smug, superior, and thoroughly intimidating.

I sat down at an empty table in a corner and nibbled on some Turkish delight, vainly hoping for invisibility. A couple soon came over to me and introduced themselves as Raven and Rue. Rue was a silent hulk of a person who sat down and stared dully at me, while Raven, small and flinching, stood behind, almost perched on Rue's shoulder, speaking into Rue's ear. The effect frightened me, as if I were eavesdropping on a deranged oracle possessed.

"She doesn't belong here," spoke Raven in a high-pitched whine. "She is wondering how to leave, but she waits for her lover who is buried in the lap of Catseye. She does not like us."

"You do not like us," echoed Rue in a flat voice. "You don't belong here."

"We must not stay long with her," continued Raven. "She is destined for pain tonight."

"Pain, pain, pain," repeated Rue, sounding almost wistful.

They both stared at me with predatory eyes. Virulent thought-forms leapt from them to me, crawling into my skin and spreading through me like a fever. At that moment, from across the room, a boy with a feral expression sunk his eyes into me. I could feel his breath on my neck. Looking away from him I saw Raven and Rue had already slunk away, stepping through a curtain to another part of the house. My heart was racing and escape my only thought.

Baptiste was enjoying the pleasures the party had to offer and was in no hurry to leave. I was afraid to leave alone and insisted he come with me. He didn't like that, though he acquiesced. He thought I was using fear to mask my jealousy and pulling a possessive power play. I admitted my jealousy, but I was angry at his insinuation that I was deceiving him or myself. Besides, I thought the party was a bad scene and couldn't understand why he'd want to stay there.

After walking a few blocks, bickering constantly, I walked away and told him to go back to the party, that I didn't need him. He was sarcastic, I was spiteful. Now my fear hid behind anger. I didn't want to admit I needed him.

Even while hurling mean words at him, part of me listened, aghast. I knew that all relationships go through ugly patches, but I thought that somehow the depth of love between Baptiste and me would make that different and even in our difficulties we would maintain dignity and respect. The possibility of misunderstanding, judgment, blame or cruelty had never occurred to me. It was a rude awakening and at that moment I became a helpless child again, lost in the war of my parents' house. I did the only thing I knew how to do.

I ran away from him, not looking back. I turned a corner to become invisible to Baptiste if he was following. I didn't know my way around the New City too well, but I didn't think I would get lost. Impulsively I turned again and headed down an alley, blinded by my anger and fear.

When someone grabbed me from behind I knew it was not Baptiste and that I was in trouble. I struggled a bit, testing my captor.

He had me tight. I relaxed into his hold, looking for an escape. Then two more boys appeared, one holding a gun. The other was the feral boy I had seen at the party. He looked mean and cold and so did his dick, which was out of his pants and pointing at me.

I was terrified. I saw no way of escape. I shit in my pants, as frightened people will do. Part of my mind managed to think about this, since it probably happens often. Does the rapist enjoy it, does it turn him on to fuck through shit? Does he inhale deeply of this tangible evidence of his power and the fear he has evoked? I was disgusted by him, but so what? At that moment, I was nothing. I had no vote.

I thought of Baptiste, looked at the glazed, drugged eyes of the boy holding the gun and prayed that Baptiste was not following. Then I saw him running towards us. A terrible feeling came over me and I knew what was about to happen even as the boy turned and fired. Five shots, then they scattered, silently, like shadows. Experienced.

Time stretched and the world lost all color as Baptiste crumpled to the ground. I saw what had been my beloved become an empty pile of non-functioning parts. I walked over to his body. It was a mess.

Picking him up and holding him in my arms, I was paralyzed for some time by my shock. A vision came to me of the Pieta, the Virgin Mary holding and mourning over the dead body of Jesus. It gave me the strength to stand up and carry Baptiste a few steps, but I realized I could not get home this way.

Nearby a man slept in a doorway, covered in cardboard and rags, oblivious to my tragedy. A shopping cart containing his belongings stood next to him. I looked through my pockets for something to trade and found Egypt's gold charm. I put it in the man's coat pocket, emptied his shopping cart, took it over to Baptiste and put him in. It was not easy. Then I started the walk to his house.

I remembered my father's death and taking him out of the city in our wheelbarrow. Though I had grieved for him, his death had been peaceful and dignified. I looked at Baptiste's body crumpled into the shopping cart, his life stolen by thugs, and my heart cried out against what had happened.

No one disturbed me on my long walk to Baptiste's house, though in the New City I passed a lot of people living on the streets.

By the time I arrived it was almost light. I looked at the stairs and wondered how I would carry Baptiste up.

As I struggled to get him out of the shopping cart, the poet appeared. How long had the poet been like this? His was an ethereal presence. When had he become this angel who now appeared to aid me? How long had it been since I heard him speak? What had happened to the man I knew? This person before me was mercy personified, silently offering his arms and his strength, taking hold of Baptiste's legs at the knees while I took him by the shoulders. Together we carried him up the stairs and inside.

Not caring about the blood, I laid him on the bed. The poet, still silent, bowed to him and to me and left. I locked the door behind him then got in the shower and washed off Baptiste's blood and my shit. When I was done I laid down next to Baptiste. Phone calls came in, messages were left, shadows moved across the floor and walls. I was dimly aware of time passing. After some hours of numbness, I wept and then, surprisingly, I slept until the next morning.

10. Transmutation

blasphemy   2. Theology. The act of claiming for oneself the attributes and rights of God.

An avalanche of postcards came through the mail slot. (Baptiste had insisted on putting it at the top of the door. He said it was harder to peep that way. I started to laugh but choked instead. Would memories always hurt this way now?) Dozens of postcards were falling in slow motion, a waterfall of pictures cascading to the floor. I picked one up - a picture of a smiling woman wearing sunglasses - and turned it over. It was from the Rev. Egypt.

"Dear Sister," it said. "Life is beautiful. Death is a mystery to be embraced when the time is right. Don't forget Jesus was murdered and rose from the dead after three days in the tomb. In the Bible His resurrection was discovered by a woman. This is only a hint. There is a power in woman that brings forth new life. This power was with Jesus for the three days. Think about this. Love, Egypt." Her words made no sense to me, but that didn't matter. I didn't really care what she was talking about.

I reached for another postcard, a picture of dakinis in the heavens. On the back was written, "Many angels here, but not you. Wish you were here. Love, Baptiste." I turned over another, a picture of angels sitting on clouds, playing harps. "Having a wonderful time. Wish we were together. All my love, Baptiste." And a third, a brightly colored picture of a laughing couple in a red convertible driving down a desert highway. A road sign read "Heavenly Highway" and on the back was written, "Holy Toledo! Where are you? Come ride shotgun! You'd love the scenery. Kisses, Baptiste."

All the rest of the cards were from Baptiste too, but I was unable to read anymore for the tears filling my eyes. Sitting on the floor surrounded by postcards from heaven, I felt dizzy and unsure where I was in relation to reality.

I walked away from the postcards, filled the tub and submerged myself in hot water. I wept, sobs that tore through my guts. I had been hallucinating. Baptiste was gone, murdered. I was not with him. He was not with me. I howled in my misery.

My grief turned to violent rage as I thought of the boy who had killed him and destroyed my life. Hating him and his cronies with all my strength, I wanted to find them, slice their dicks off, chop off their heads, rip out their hearts, sever their limbs, cut the pieces into smaller pieces and toss them all in a dumpster. My blood sang with heat and I felt powerful, capable of murder and vengeance. I was out of the tub and into my clothes in moments, high on my venom.

While heading towards the door, my collection of fragrant oils caught my eye. My arm reached out and knocked them all off their shelf. They had no purpose now. I had shared them with Baptiste. The sounds of bottles falling and breaking was satisfying to my rage.

Then I saw myself in the mirror. The wild grief and naked insanity in my reflection frightened me, propelling me into grabbing the mirror and hurling it to the floor, screaming, then crumpling to the floor, whimpering. I couldn't kid myself. I couldn't go out and take on a gang of thugs. I probably couldn't even make it out of the house. Not only that, what was the point? It wouldn't bring Baptiste back. He wouldn't be with me again.

The shattered mirror called out to me. I couldn't bring him back to me, so I would go to him. Picking up a piece, I tried to concentrate and remember what I had been told was the most effective way of doing this.

The Rev. Egypt wrapped her arms around me from behind, pulling the mirror out of my hand as she did so. How had she come in? I turned into her embrace and wept while she held me for a long, long time.

When I looked up into the innocence that was her face, all else was momentarily forgotten. The full moon of her face, the sphinx slant of her eyes, the softness of her mouth, the thick black cascade of her hair was fully revealed to me for the first time, instantly imprinted on my soul, and immediately familiar and beloved.

She led me into the back room and held me in the sunlight, kissing my tears. I wanted her to heal me, to make my pain go away, to rewrite the past. I wanted the truth to be different: I wanted her to bring Baptiste back to me. When I told her all this, she stroked my cheek and murmured, "Peace. Be still. The future is still unwritten."

Egypt had brought me many powerful experiences, precipitated by the mere sound of her voice or the glance of her eyes. To now feel her hair touching mine and her hand lightly on my cheek was frightening in its intensity. My thinking mind fought her presence; after all, my lover had just been killed. My thinking mind, however, was not in control of this situation.

My cheek burned in the place her hand had been. She kissed me on the mouth, then withdrew about an inch. I breathed her in and the fragrance of her touched my lungs. She rubbed her cheek against mine as if we were kittens, then with tiny serpentine movements entwined our bodies and held me captive. Even as my body responded to her, I was terrified. This was the woman who had melted into the fire and returned. She would annihilate me with her potency.

My body sang out: could I resist such a glorious opportunity?

She kissed me again and I learned the language of her mouth, her tongue and teeth. Her hair tumbled over us and tickled me. She leaned back, laughing. In her strong white teeth I saw the tigress that would relentlessly tear away all barriers between us, exposing my flesh to its depths. She pounced on me, sending both my fear and our clothes flying.

In her eyes waited the falcon that would seize me in its talons and take me high above the earth, while in the rise and fall of her belly moved the serpent that transfixed me. I beheld in her triangle of tiny black curls the sphinx and the feeling roused in me was the riddle.

I remembered Baptiste. I covered my eyes with my hands and, curling into a little ball, fought for some ground to hold on to. What was happening was impossible. She kissed my forehead and said in a voice of prayer, "Give up your faith in death. Give up your faith in pain. Surrender it all to the Mystery," while she continued to kiss and caress me. Once again it didn't seem strange that we would be making love while Baptiste's body lay cold and still in the other room.

Running my hands through the fields of her hair, running my tongue through the moist cavern of her mouth, all the desire I had ever felt for her was rising in me, filling my guts, my blood, my limbs, pounding at the gate of my pleasure. I wanted to bury myself in her, forget myself in her, lose myself in her soul.

Then it all started to seem wrong again and she gentled me with her hands. I thought I might be going insane but any time that idea came Egypt caressed me and it was as if she was caressing my mind, gently brushing that thought away.

"Yes," her encouraging whisper made no outside sound as it echoed down the corridor of my bones. "In you is the power of life, death, and resurrection. Deny no possibility, accept no limit, most holy one."

To be visited by love, sex, and death concurrently, to feel so intensely both desire and grief, was plunging me into chaos. Egypt's gentle breath somehow guided my mind until I touched Baptiste in thought and felt his presence. My heart was comforted. I understood that there was life and love beyond this reality and that our separation was illusory. I blessed Egypt for this healing and this communion.

"Blessed be the Mystery, blessed be the keeper of the Mystery. Come to me, most holy one, my dove, my precious one," she sang inside my heart.

My flesh rippled and streamed around her as if I were the desert sand and her breath and hands the wind. She rested her hand above my heart and the warmth of her touch flowed out over my breasts and travelled beneath and below, into my breastbone and ribs, spreading through my vertebrae and down into the girdle of my pelvis. Never had I thought of bones as capable of arousal, but she woke them from their virginal slumber into an unexpected sensitivity. My body joined Egypt's in its sinuous fluidity.

We opened the precious gate and travelled through mysterious caverns and valleys, explored the grotto of the white tiger, dallied in the valley of joy, and reveled in the pleasure fields of heaven. Our upper mouths led the kisses and our lower mouths followed, kissing and sucking the nectar from each other, kissing and coming, coming and kissing.

We soared with the magnificent phoenix. Enthralled by the beauty of the lotus flower, we adored the precious crucible. Hands and tongues caressed and opened the insides of mouths, yonis and the tender little flower that is the yoni's close friend.

The world melted away, replaced by an aura of brilliant color all around us, rosy gold and lapis blue. Egypt's eyes were gateways into the heavens. Time and space became irrelevant. She fed me all the beauty of the universe with her hand inside my adoring cunt.

Oh Egypt, into your hands I commend my spirit.

It was as if I were birthing her or she was birthing me, a feeling of being opened by something as instinctual and uncontrollable as the birth rhythm. Torn open, at times painful, pain yielding to orgasm, orgasm yielding to yet more opening in the center of our flesh, in the cervix, in the womb, the heart and home of humanity. Tearing it open to let life out, to let life in, to let life through. Groaning in bringing down God through the womb of woman. Tearing open until there was nothing left but a sound, a great sound, a cosmic orgasm, a reverberating prayer, the Word, the triumphant howling scream of a woman who has lost all trace of civilization, taken into the ecstatic baptism of the ocean of mercy.

Following the ebb and flow of that ocean, I eventually found myself once more feeling the boundary of my flesh, the wild holiness of cosmic orgasm tranquilly encompassed in the more familiar pulsations of heartbeat and breath. It was as Egypt had said that first day at the Oxygen Feather: "It can be as simple as this: open and close, back and forth, empty and full, expand and contract, the rhythm of breath, heartbeat, lovemaking, life. Know this and you can know everyone and everything."

I was at peace with Baptiste's death. I knew my grieving was not complete and that pain would return, but that this peace would be there to hold me. I knew my anger was not finished and that this too I could hold with my peace. Then Egypt whispered in my ear, "Did you get my postcard?"

I got up and walked out to the hall, Egypt following. They were still there, a pile of postcards on the floor. It was all real. "Jesus spent three days in the tomb, then rose from the dead," she murmured. "It can happen whenever conditions are right and a woman is willing."

"Are you saying Baptiste will rise from the dead?" I asked.

"No," she answered.

I was relieved but somehow disappointed. Life having lost all parameters of what I considered normal, why not have Baptiste get up and walk out of the other room?

"I did not say Baptiste will rise from the dead," she continued, "but Baptiste could be resurrected if you are willing."

Once again the idea of insanity came up, but now I thought it was Egypt, not me. She brushed that thought away as if it were a fly.

I gave in. "What do I do?" I asked.

"Make love to him. Visit the world beyond and bring him back. Let yourself dissolve and rebirth him through the power in your womb and in your heart. Ask Jesus to help you." She kissed me, then turned and walked away.

I stepped into the other room, feeling numb. Baptiste was laid out on the bed. Who had taken off his clothes and washed the blood off him? Who had cleaned his face and laid him on top of our red blanket? Who had filled the room with candles and lit them all?

Baptiste was bathed in the warm, golden glow of the candlelight.

We were both naked, Baptiste laying on the bed, and I, standing in the doorway, looking down at him, still wet and dishevelled from loving Egypt. I wanted to turn around and go back to her. He was dead and our relationship was over. I grieved for him, but strong in my heart was my love for Egypt, a love that had always existed side by side with my love for Baptiste.

Why had she sent me back here? Certainly what she had been saying had been intended as an obscure metaphor that I as yet failed to understand.

What was I to do with a dead man?

I sat down, got quiet inside and contemplated the body of Baptiste for some time. My instinctive self grew stronger and gained ascendancy over my thinking mind. It came to me that what I was about to do was written into my destiny as surely as my love for him and Egypt had been. He could have been asleep, his staff erect the way it often was just before he woke up. He was my beloved.

I hesitate a moment and then kneel at his feet, touching them, then kissing them. This is an okay thing to do, even if he is dead. It's a way of honoring the body that held the spirit of my beloved. I don't even have to think about the things Egypt said. And then I do think about what Egypt said and remember why I am here.

A moment of fear, a moment of panic and I forget to breathe. A moment of gasping, grasping for air, feeling life in me, in my breath, in my heartbeat, in my thinking and in my sensing. A moment of paralysis and then I touch him with my whole body laid out against his, his body which doesn't breathe, doesn't beat, doesn't sense me there. A moment of disgust and I move myself away again.

A moment of confusion and a sense of blasphemy. I feel nauseous, dizzy, and frightened. I understand that I am about to commit blasphemy but I do not know what blasphemy is. I laugh but then the laughter is choked by grief. A moment of disowning myself, of washing my hands of it all and then I call on Jesus to help me.

He is there as quick as thought. We speak no words to each other but his gentle eyes embrace and encourage me. He puts my hand on his sacred heart and gives me a cup of his blood to drink to banish my fear. He kisses my forehead and blesses me, then he is gone.

A memory visits me from the early days of my love with Baptiste. We were lounging together in the bath and he was massaging the inside of my mouth with two of his fingers, which was highly arousing to me. I asked where he had acquired such skill and he replied,"I do with you what I am compelled to do." This memory fortifies me, as I am now compelled to fuck a dead man for a holy purpose.

I lay down with Baptiste and kiss his hair, his eyes, his ears, his mouth, blessing and loving the face that rests there unused, discarded, but still somehow part of my beloved. I kiss the bullet holes in his forehead, chest, and belly, my tenderness overflowing with pain. I hold him and am surprised to feel passion stirring and taking possession of me, a flame whose single purpose is to find and encompass Baptiste.

My hands and mouth lovingly explore Baptiste's body, searching for the door upon which to knock, seeking passage to Baptiste, asking Infinite Spirit to illuminate the path. When I take his penis into my hands and guide it into my phoenix, it is with full reverence for the sacrament I understand this to be.

An angel with a flaming sword approaches me and with one stroke, severs my head. My blood showers Baptiste; his mouth opens and his tongue laps at my blood. The room disappears. I find myself in a sunny meadow, Baptiste running ahead of me, both of us whole, vibrant and free.

I run towards him on winged feet, as fleet as a wild horse and then my way is blocked by a line of men. I remember them all and my heart hardens:

there, the tortured, sensitive, soul and

there, the one who told me how it was going to be and

there, the one who wouldn't be my friend if he couldn't be my lover and

there, the one who needed just a little more time and

there, the one who told me I'd get used to it and

there, the one who couldn't pick on someone his own size and

there, the one who travelled 3,000 miles to haunt me and

there, the one who swore to kill me if he couldn't have me and

there, the one who was going to stop drinking soon and

there, the one who slapped me inside a church and told me I didn't know how to pray and

there, the one who scarred my cunt and

there, the one who put the needle in me and

there, the one who tried to rape me and

there, the one who fired the bullets into Baptiste and next to them the angel weeps and I taste bitterness. Baptiste is gone and I'm back in his room. I am filled with rage and then I feel Baptiste's cold body and I can't believe what I have been doing so I throw myself off the bed in disgust and pace the house, my heart filled with violence.

In the kitchen I come upon the Rev. Egypt and Jesus Christ, sitting together at the table, drinking tea. I want them to go away. I want everything to go away. Jesus offers me a seat with an elegant gesture of his hand. Why do holy people always have such beautiful hands and such graceful movements? Grudgingly, I sit down.

"I know this is hard for you," Jesus says as he takes my hand. His voice is the most beautiful sound that has ever existed on this earth. Tears fill my eyes but already I feel better. He has that power. He's every best friend I've ever wished for.

"I failed." I confess to him.

"Ego severance is not easy. Letting go is not easy. There is no failure in discovering how dearly you love your pain. "

He hold out his arms to me and lets me cry in them.

"It's just so complicated," I babble as I come out of his embrace. My statement sounds inane to my ears, but he takes it just as I say it.

"When things become complicated, simplify. Let's start by going back to the Holy Breath. Lay everything else aside, just for now. "

We breathe together for a few minutes, the three of us. Egypt's perfumed presence is a comfort. The inside of my body is still whirling, but I begin to feel my feet on the floor, my hand in Jesus '. A little while longer, and I begin to feel calm, just breathing, breathing with the Rev. Egypt and Jesus Christ while sitting on a chair in Baptiste's kitchen.

"Good," he says. "And now, go a little deeper. Continue with the Holy Breath, but exclude nothing. Let everything in. Hold it all in the cauldron of your belly. "

I do as he says and at first I feel as if overcome by a hurricane, all my fury and fear rushing in to take control. Jesus calms me with the sound of his voice and the touch of his hand. I remember the story in the Bible where he calmed the waves of the stormy sea. The power of his love, his gentle, defenseless, all-encompassing love, emanates from him.

I let it carry me for a while, and at some point I realize I am walking on the water of my emotions, the water calm, my mind calm, and yet it is all still there; Baptiste, the rapists, every painful experience of my life, still and calm inside my belly.

Jesus touches my breast with his hand. A warmth travels from my belly to my heart, and my flesh lets him pass. His hand passes through my skin and through my breastbone until his fingers briefly rest upon my heart itself, a place never before touched. Tears cascade from my eyes: Jesus Christ has opened my heart with his hand. The world pauses in silent exhilaration; I feel the Holy Breath inhaling and exhaling the entire planet.

"This is a great initiation for you," Jesus says. "A whole religion was created out of my resurrection 2000 years ago, but I did not resurrect myself. It is the power of woman that gives birth. Woman can give re-birth as well. Woman is the bridge between heaven and earth, between life and death."

He laughs heartily.

"It is a pity that this great power has become such a great taboo. Well, my dear, you just have to trust us." He stands up and takes my hand, still chuckling. Egypt takes my other hand and together they lead me back to the other room. Angels surround Baptiste in the candlelight, holding him as if he were a child, singing unknown lullabies.

I don't want to admit to Jesus and Egypt that I am afraid, that I still don't want to believe all this is happening, that I don't want to see or touch Baptiste again. Right now I would prefer to bury him and be done with it. I'd like to go and live alone in the desert for a while and forget all this.

All through my childhood my secret ambition had been to become a saint. I wanted to heal my family and everyone I knew. I wanted the Divine protection and approval that sainthood would confer upon me. Now two people have brought me a new image of God to replace the one of God the Father that wore out so long ago. The Rev. Egypt is surely a saint and Jesus is holy beyond sainthood, and yet I cannot bring myself to continue along this path they have set me on. I feel sad, guilty, and ashamed, but I want them to go away and leave me alone.

"You may go anywhere you wish," Egypt whispers tenderly in

my ear. "All channels are open to you. You may go to the desert, you may go beyond the veil, you may go to hell."

I turn around, shocked to hear her last words, which I have only ever heard as a curse, but both Egypt and Jesus are gone. I'm relieved. I don't want to think about anything for awhile.

11. Resurrection

"Nothing shall be impossible for you." (Matthew 17:20)

Sitting in the kitchen, sipping hot tea, I feel somewhat calm. My experiences with Jesus and Egypt are starting to fade as dreams will and that is good. It means I am connecting back with reality after experiencing a temporary loss of sanity due to my shock and grief. That is natural. Now I am coming to terms with reality. That too is natural. There is a natural progression to life's traumas. I will follow its course. It is part of life.

My last night with Baptiste was filled with dissent, quarreling, and anger. I was violent with the man I loved, attacking his spirit with my uncontrolled emotions. Now he was gone and I could never atone.

This realization sat in my belly like a stone. I wept and this feeling was familiar to me, having failed so many times in life and made so many mistakes. No matter how many times I tried to pull myself up with lofty spiritual ideas, this grey zone was my true home, the only place I believed in. This was real, this hopeless place that I could never really leave behind, no matter how many times I pretended to.

Truly I was the one to blame for Baptiste's death and all my hallucinations had been my mind's way of keeping me from coming face to face with that fact. I could blame the boy with the gun, but who had opened the way to violence with her venomous spirit? Who had turned us into targets? Who had run thoughtlessly through unknown streets? Who had learned decades ago to always be vigilant in the world? Was I not a woman?

Life had been more beautiful than anything I could have imagined, but I had been unable to sustain it. The demons in my heart had sent Baptiste away. If I had only known just how far away I would send him. If I had only known where my anger would take us.

Foolishly indulging my petty spite, I had initiated a chain of circumstances that took my lover's life. Now there was nothing I could do, despite these wild imaginings of resurrection and Jesus Christ rising from the dead through the power of sex. Denial could only last so long. Baptiste was dead and I was to blame. There was nothing else to say and no one to save me.

A dangerous voice slithered into my mind and whispered seductively to me: "Your self-pity, I must say, is boring and uninspired. Your self-accusations have no originality. Insipid is your personal hell, completely lacking in artistry. I can show you much, much more. Permit me."

My spirit is seized and trapped by a moment of undiluted hell. A moment of flames that devours the cloak of my self-pity, a moment that tears me apart, a moment where the memory of paradise vanishes utterly from my soul, a moment that screams.

A moment of rape by random thoughtforms, of penetration by demons. A moment without oxygen, a moment of being buried alive, burned at the stake, betrayed by someone I love.

A moment of starvation, a moment of implosion, a moment of molecular annihilation. A moment of mutating cells, a moment of melting in a radioactive flood.

A moment of delirium, a moment that shuts its eyes, a moment of terror as vast as night.

A moment of trial by jury, a moment that fails me, a moment that eternally pierces my heart with lies. A moment of blood, a moment that weeps, a moment that wears my mother's face.

Down in the dust on my belly, I am naked under a burning desert sun. Whenever I try to get up a strong force, like a demon's foot, presses on my back and pushes me into the dust. I hear a crunching sound as vertebrae after vertebrae is stepped on and smashed. I crawl on my belly in the dirt as my back is alternately broken and healed to the rhythm of my agonized breath. I arrive at the shore of a sea of barbed wire. I am not permitted to turn or rise, I must crawl on my belly through barbed wire, my flesh ripping open, tearing raw and bleeding like my mind. There is no protection for me. I had thought my skin would always be able to cover me, whole and safe. I thought my mind would always be my own.

A rain of blood pours down, the smell of it engulfing me, a storm raining all the blood that has ever been spilled in the war. A moment of vomiting that blood. A derelict moment wailing with regret, devoid of vision, squeezing out all hope, a moment that shatters into infinite mirrors of pain.

I am strapped down on a table while the hands of two men reach into me to pull out my stillborn child. They are sarcastic and joking. I can't stand the feel of their hands inside me, their rough, unkind hands. I want to close my legs against them but the drugs they have given me have temporarily paralyzed me from the waist down. I look at all the blood on the floor and hope I won't have to clean it up.

They put the baby on my belly and leave me alone under the bright lights, laughing as they exit. I touch the infant that has no life. Its face is my own.

I know this onslaught will never stop and though I cannot bear it I know I will be unable to ever lose consciousness.

It is hardly audible, a faint chant: "holy breath, sacred heart. holy breath, sacred heart." In the midst of hell, I find my body and am able to draw one breath, I am able to hear for one second the beat of my heart and then I find myself back in Baptiste's house, a house on fire. Walking through flames to the room where Baptiste lies, I lay down and cling to him, nailing myself to my cross, my cross that is Baptiste.

The flames make my eyes burn and tear. The lack of oxygen causes me to fight for each breath and I am afraid that my flesh will melt but I hold tight to my lover and find myself transported back to the meadow, where I find myself immediately surrounded by a mob. Some of the faces are familiar: Father Jacobson, my parents, my brother who disowned me when I was born, ex-lovers, housemates and friends, even the poet.

All of them caution me that my intentions are perverse, sick, sinful, disgusting, injurious to my mental health and perilous to my immortal soul. They beg me to reconsider; they turn their backs in disgust; they throw stones and curse me. They tell me I will have no place among them if I do this.

Battered by the stones and their rejection, I am momentarily overcome by fear and confusion. An image of Jesus comes into my mind, reminding me that the Holy Breath and Sacred Heart delivered me from hell. I know it was all real, everything that happened with Jesus and Egypt, that other women have walked this road for the love of Christ and that I can do the same. This acceptance destroys the illusion: I have been walking through a field of phantoms, inhabited by my own projections, peopled by remnants of war still clinging to my mind.

Walking through the meadow, I arrive at the bank of a river, a bloody river of broken hearts. I want to gather them up but my arms cannot hold them in their slippery bloodiness. Something in me demands that I eat and drink.

"This is my body, this is my blood."

Choking on the first tastes, I retch, vomit, and cry. It is difficult but I eat and drink and finally I swallow one heart. It says "thank

129

you" to me so I want to continue eating but I cannot bring myself to eat more flesh and blood. A heart leaps out of the river and clings to me like a leech. It has little hands and a mouth with teeth with which it rips open my chest, yanks out my heart and throws it in the river. Now I must eat all the hearts and drink all the blood in order to find my own heart. There is no other way.

I step into the slippery, warm river, knee deep in blood and hearts. My hands are bloody as I scoop up the hearts. I put my mouth to the bloody river and drink. I eat and I drink; my face, my hair, my hands are bloody. It's difficult to stay steady, and I fall in from time to time, baptized in blood.

I eat and I drink; my stomach gets full and then my womb opens and reaches up to take the hearts, growing and expanding to hold them all. My womb knows how to nurture them, nourish them, return them to wholeness and birth them all into freedom.

I realize this is woman's work and a woman's work is never done.

When I eat my own heart it tastes no different than any of the others. I only know it to be mine because it settles under my breast instead of into my womb. The blood I have drunk, the blood of humanity, dances in my veins. The hearts birthed by my womb, the hearts of humanity, sing to me with their gentled rhythm.

The place where Jesus touched my heart burns, asking for my memories of hell and the fear and anger of a lifetime. I allow them all to go to the altar of my heart and feel the transforming flame of my Sacred Heart set ablaze, nourishing and purifying me. There is no war left in me, only the sweetest peace.

The voice of Jesus whispers in my ear the true words he spoke on the cross, giving me the ambrosia of heaven, the oxygen of the soul. I feel the arousing power of my womb and I breathe deeply into it. My heart is a magnet for the presence of God and I no longer restrain it.

I look out over what was once the river of broken hearts, where the water now runs clear. In front of me old stone steps lead down into the river. The body of Baptiste floats on a raft in its quiet waters, covered with and surrounded by fragrant flowers. I step out into the river to adore his body.

Tenderly kissing his mouth, I feel all the love that Baptiste bestowed upon me through these lips, with his kisses and his whispered words. His soul no longer speaks through this mouth, but something remains, an after-image perhaps, or the taste of a memory.

The fragrance of the flowers is reminiscent of our nights in the gardens. Dreamily I make love to Baptiste. I feel the echo of his soul through the flowers, the water, and his body. Once he was inside this body, now he is dispersed into everything. I do not immediately notice that the water is pulling me down. Lost in my mood, I accept it as an embrace from Baptiste.

When I am completely submerged, I come to in a panic, fighting for air. The voice of the water says, "Peace. Be still." It is as irresistible as gravity, but something in me continues to fight for individual life and survival. Sinking deeper into the water, into a cool dark stillness, everything is included, loved and cherished in this Celestial River, a tributary of the universal Ocean of Mercy.

My heart offers itself in peace and my body ceases its struggle. Life is an inhalation, death an exhalation in this River of Infinite Spirit. I accept water into my lungs and allow myself to dissolve into its primeval depths. One by one my thoughts and emotions are extinguished in the stillness like clothes put aside for the pure moment of a naked embrace.

The rising sun opens my eyes, its rays sinking deeply into the body I seem to inhabit. Am I alive or dead? It doesn't matter. I don't need an address or a definition. There is awareness; I don't know where that awareness comes from.

There is ground that I lie upon. The sun traverses the sky; something responds in me. The sun sets and the moon rises; something yearns in me. My identity awakens and my body is full of Grace. I have lost my life and found it; I have been baptized in the River of Life More Abundant and re-born in the womb of the Ocean of Mercy. Life sings in me and a purpose tugs at me. When I see a fire burning in the distance, instinct takes me there. This is the culmination of my journey: Baptiste's funeral pyre.

Climbing the ladder onto the pyre, the heat and power of the fire encircle me like a healing aura of light. Before me lie the skeletal remains of Baptiste. Laughter bubbles out of me from someplace I did not know before.

The Holy Breath is alive with power in me. The flames of the pyre are as exhilarating as pure mountain air, as comfortable as clear, warm, buoyant sea water, as nourishing as desert solitude. I am at home in the heart of the fire, transformed by the power in me. Just as a woman can only access the power to give birth when her time has come, so my time is come to give re-birth to Baptiste.

Alone with this power, with the fire, with Baptiste, I squat over him, drawing him into my eager phoenix, performing an act that I never knew was possible, much less something programmed into my genes, as much a part of nature as is procreation. I breathe fire into my lungs and then release the Holy Breath over Baptiste. His flesh returns when my breath touches him. Mesmerized by this miraculous sight, I behold the supernatural beauty of his new flesh blossoming into existence and covering his bones.

This terrain is beyond all my dreams. Kissing Baptiste's reborn flesh in awe, caressing him with my intoxicated breath, my exhilarated body trembles. I am Venus surfing the waves of bliss, Kali riding the waves of the Ocean of Mercy. Between my legs is a chalice of life and the wisdom imprinted in every cell of my cunt initiates me into a hidden dimension of sharing that chalice in the holy communion of sex.

Milking him with the birth rhythm of my cunt, the life rhythm of my breath, and the love rhythm of my beating heart, my cunt drips with passion and his staff awakens when the river flowing from me anoints it. The new life of him, erect and throbbing, burning with the essence of life, touches my womb, my lower heart.

My tongue drips with passion and my saliva lands on Baptiste's face. His eyes open when my saliva touches them. His lips of myrrh open when my saliva touches them. Bending down, my tongue dripping with passion, I kiss him deeply. His lungs open when my breath enters his body. In my excitement I bite my lips and his. My lips, swollen and bloody with passion, press his and his heart begins to beat when his blood mingles with mine.

Moving off of him, I stretch out and cover him with my hands, my breath, and my kisses. Without restraint I rub myself against him, ever deepening my rapture, anointing him with the passion dripping from my two mouths. His limbs awaken and his arms reach out for me. He clings to me, almost born. At this moment, I am all life to him.

I release myself to the Power coursing through me. I abandon myself to the Power that rides on the wings of the Holy Breath and gives substance to the nectar flowing from my body. My phoenix swoops down to again seize my beloved and fly away with him, for the Mystery is in possession of us, transporting us to a place of freedom beyond life and death, where Baptiste's spirit awakens into my embrace.

The gods and goddesses, laughing with delight as we meld together in our rapture, let us join them for a brief eternity in their sacred orgy. They let us join them in the divine lovemaking that puts the stars in the sky and the fire in the sun and the mystery in the hearts of humanity. They let us join them in their holy communion and feel for an infinite second the passion of the cosmos, but we are only man and woman. We surrender into oblivion.

I regain consciousness in our bed, Baptiste laying in my arms, our cozy blankets covering us, the sun streaming in, and a radiant Rev. Egypt crossing the room toward us bearing a tray holding three crystal goblets filled with water and wine.

12. Destination

"I have said, Ye are gods; and all of you are children of the Most High." (Psalm 82:6, John 10:34)

Egypt took care of us after our miraculous three days and remained with us for forty days and forty nights. She had been teacher, priestess, friend, catalyst, lover, and now mother to us, gliding into this new role with her usual dexterity, grace, and whole-hearted enthusiasm. She nurtured us through our re-born, new-born time as we gradually acclimatized to the world.

Initially we were quite giddy with it all. Baptiste teased me endlessly. If I had been able to resurrect him, had I not also the power to give him a right hand? I teased him back : his hand was no longer available as personal; it had merged with the universal hand of protection, hand of blessing, hand of healing. I remember those days as a heady mix of laughter, awe, and boundless love. I experienced the world freshly created every moment. The Infinite Spirit of Love was alive in everything! I wanted to shout from the rooftops.

Egypt celebrated with us while gently guiding us, helping us to integrate our miraculous experiences into our lives. My mind was filled with the question "Why?" Why had we been given this gift? Why me? Why Baptiste? Why resurrection?

"Resurrection served your evolution, nothing more and certainly nothing less," Egypt replied. "Jesus was crucified and resurrected to serve his evolution and the evolution of his companions, but he had cast his net wider than that. His purpose was to touch and evolve the hearts of all humanity.

"Resurrection is not the path for the few nor for all. There are many ways to embrace the Mystery. Impress this upon your heart: there are as many paths to the Infinite Spirit as there are stars in the sky. The world often chooses to see differences as reason for conflict. Use the eyes of your spirit and you will see in differences only the multi-faceted glory of God."

The poet had told people on the farm that Baptiste had kidnapped me in a fit of passion, so no one worried about us and since the harvest was over, few were bothered by our taking unrequested time off.

I was a little apprehensive when I first left the seclusion of Baptiste's house. Had our experience left some visible trace on me, a stigma whereby everyone would know what we had done? I was afraid that people would alternately lust after me and fear me. I was soon able to laugh over that fear. Baptiste's resurrection remained a secret, though people did notice and comment on the aura of love around us.

It was rare for Egypt to speak of herself, but one afternoon she did.

"My teacher was Edison Spark," she mentioned in an almost casual way, a look of fond reminiscence on her face.

I remembered the name. Edison Spark was the artist responsible for the Guardian's Gate and the Plague Wall. She saw the surprise in my face and nodded.

" Yes, Edison did die of the plague. His death had all the glory of Baptiste's resurrection. Resurrection is not a way to avoid death and thinking that way would not be desirable. Jesus himself only remained with his companions for forty days after his resurrection before ascending to heaven.

"In life there is death and in death there is life. To live fully, one has to constantly let go of all that has gone before. Once we stop interpreting the world we can begin to truly interact with it. Everyday the false must die so the true can live.

"I was one of the people who helped Edison construct the Gate and the Wall. That project was the beginning of my discipleship with him. We spent two years in the desert together after that. He had several other students with him, but not many. He was not a teacher for the multitudes. After his death, his disciples split up, each to our own way. I continued my wandering in the desert and he continued to teach me after his death. Both he and Jesus appeared to me often, until I was free of doubt and ready to begin my ministry. When I came to the city it was to find you.

"You see, I also made love with Edison the same way you made love with Baptiste. The difference was, Edison did not intend to come back. But he awakened me so I in turn could awaken you and you will, at the right time, awaken others."

Awaiting Further Instructions from the Most High

It has been two and a half years since we last saw Egypt. I got a postcard from the Rev. recently, a picture of two lovers embracing on a flying carpet. It said:

"Write down your story. Call out to others. There are more of you than you know. I have been busy since we parted and soon I will have the opportunity to return to the city and be with you again. My love to you all. I am filled with eagerness to see the child. Perhaps I will sprout wings to hasten my journey! Egypt."

I looked over at Rosary Sahara, careening down the hall, doing the toddler shuffle-run with a big grin on her face. Given the unusual circumstances of her conception, I can't help at times but wonder what her destiny will be. I love to watch her, to see the delight she feels in life shining through her face, her body, her every movement. I, too, was eager for them to meet and to see Egypt again. In the meantime, she had given me this task: to write down this memoir, this confession, this love letter.

I felt feverish as I began to write, pictures of memory chasing each other through my brain, tumbling and melting into the sights and sounds outside me. The yellow of the tulips on my desk leapt into my mouth and fed me, the song of the woman across the street entered my blood and moved me. How sweet to have no defense from my environment. These years that I have been aware of the Holy Breath, these years since Baptiste's resurrection, I have lived with a secret and now I would tell it. I would tell of having heaven between my legs, of the consuming fire of passion in my sacred heart, and my words would stream from my mouth like incense, drifting up to the Most High.

I wrote this all down in privacy; perhaps you now read it in privacy. We are separated by time in the giving and the receiving of the story but, as you read this and always, we are together in the Holy Breath.

To all my friends, lovers, and enemies , past, present, and future: I'll meet you there.

Walk through the doorway.